I0663271

MEDITATIONS OF DESCARTES

A Ground-Breaking Exploration of Reason, Existence & the Nature of Reality

A Modern Translation
Adapted for the Contemporary Reader

René Descartes

Translated by Tim Zengerink

© **Copyright 2025. All rights reserved.**

It is not legal to reproduce, duplicate, or transmit any part of this document in either electronic means or in printed format. Recording of this publication is strictly prohibited and any storage of this document is not allowed unless with written permission from the publisher except for the use of brief quotations in a book review

TABLE OF CONTENTS

PREFACE
MESSAGE TO THE READER

Rebuilding the Greatest Library in Human History

Thousands of years ago, the Library of Alexandria was the heart of global knowledge — a sanctuary where the wisdom of every known civilization was gathered and shared freely.

And then, it was lost.

Now, we're rebuilding it — and you are invited to join us.

At the Library of Alexandria, we've set out to make every book available to every person on Earth — not just in print, but in every language, every format, and for every reader.

Here's how we do it:

- **Deluxe Print Editions at True Printing Cost** - Order any book as a high-quality paperback, elegant hardcover, or stunning boxset — and only pay what it costs to print. No markups. No middlemen.
- **Unlimited Access to the Greatest Works** - Enjoy thousands of timeless classics — from Plato to Shakespeare to Tolstoy — in beautiful, modern eBook and audiobook editions. Read and listen without limits — for every reader, everywhere.
- **Modern Translations for Every Language & Dialect** - We're reimagining the classics in clear, accessible language — and translating them into every dialect imaginable. Everyone deserves to understand humanity's greatest ideas.

When you visit **LibraryofAlexandria.com**, you're not just accessing books — you're joining a global movement to restore, preserve, and share the wisdom of civilization.

Join us today at LibraryofAlexandria.com

Together, we'll ensure the light of human wisdom never fades again.

With gratitude,

The Modern Library of Alexandria Team

Visit:
www.libraryofalexandria.com
Or scan the code below:

INTRODUCTION

DESCARTES THE REVOLUTIONARY: A NEW METHOD FOR KNOWING

In the vast landscape of Western philosophy, few thinkers have left a deeper and more enduring mark than René Descartes. Known as the father of modern philosophy, Descartes dared to discard centuries of inherited belief in pursuit of absolute certainty. His work *Meditations on First Philosophy*, published in Latin in 1641, stands as a monumental effort to rebuild the foundations of knowledge from the ground up. With boldness, clarity, and logical rigor, Descartes asked: *What can I know for certain?* And from that question arose a whole new philosophical era.

Born in 1596 in France, Descartes lived at a time when the old certainties of religion, science, and scholastic philosophy were crumbling under the pressure of new discoveries and new doubts. The Renaissance had awakened a thirst for knowledge; the Reformation had fractured the religious unity of Europe; and the Scientific Revolution had begun to shift humanity's view of the universe from a divine order to a mechanical one. In this intellectual upheaval, Descartes sought a firm foundation for truth—one that would be immune to skepticism, dogma, and error.

The Meditations is the record of that quest. It is a journey inward, into the mind of the philosopher, stripped of all assumptions, beliefs, and sensory impressions. Its structure is deceptively simple: six meditations, written as if over six days, in which Descartes resolves to doubt everything he thinks he knows until he arrives at a truth that cannot be doubted. From that first certainty—*Cogito, ergo sum* ("I think, therefore I am")—he rebuilds a system of knowledge that encompasses the soul, God, and the material world.

But this is no dry exercise in metaphysics. Descartes' *Meditations* is a profound human document—a work of existential courage, intellectual solitude, and spiritual struggle. It is the cry of a man who seeks light in a world of shadows, and it invites the reader into the same quest. In an age obsessed with information, *The Meditations* calls us back to *understanding*. It demands not just belief, but justification; not just knowledge, but certainty.

Descartes' method would become the foundation for much of modern philosophy, mathematics, and science. His emphasis on doubt, methodical reasoning, and the autonomy of the thinking subject would shape thinkers from Spinoza to Kant, from Hume to Heidegger. Even today, debates about consciousness, mind-body dualism, and the limits of empirical knowledge trace their roots to Descartes' deceptively small volume of meditations.

To read *Meditations on First Philosophy* is to encounter a turning point in human thought—a moment when reason stepped boldly into the unknown and dared to find order not in tradition or authority, but in the clarity of its own light.

DOUBT, CERTAINTY, AND THE FOUNDATIONS OF KNOWLEDGE

At the heart of Descartes' meditations is a radical method of doubt. Descartes does not begin with a claim—he begins with a demolition. He resolves to doubt everything he has ever believed: the evidence of the senses, the truths of mathematics, the teachings of authorities. Even the most basic beliefs—like the existence of a physical world—are not immune. Why? Because they might be false. Because they might be dreams. Because, just possibly, a malevolent demon is deceiving him at every turn.

This famous "evil demon" hypothesis is not just a philosophical gimmick. It's a tool—an extreme test designed to strip away anything that is not absolutely indubitable. And it works. Descartes shows that nearly everything we think we know could, in theory, be wrong. Except one thing: the fact that he is *thinking*. No matter how much he doubts, the very act of doubting proves that he exists—at least as a thinking thing. *Cogito, ergo sum.*

From this one certainty, Descartes begins to rebuild. If he is a thinking thing, then thought exists. But what of the soul? The body? The external world? Descartes proceeds with caution, analyzing the nature of ideas and how they appear in the mind. He argues that some ideas—like the idea of God—are so perfect and infinite that they could not have originated from himself. Therefore, they must have been placed in him by something real—something perfect. This leads Descartes to argue for the existence of a benevolent God, who would not deceive him about the nature of reality.

With God as the guarantor of truth, Descartes feels he can once again trust clear and distinct perceptions. This allows him to re-establish belief in the material world, the laws of nature, and even the existence of the body. But crucially, he does so from within the mind—not by appealing to external evidence, but by deducing from first principles.

This method—rationalism—sets Descartes apart from empirical thinkers like John Locke and David Hume, who emphasized sensory experience. Descartes insists that the mind is primary, and that reason alone can provide the foundations of science, ethics, and theology. In doing so, he sets the stage for centuries of debate about the nature and limits of human knowledge.

But the Meditations are more than abstract arguments. They are also a personal record of philosophical struggle. Descartes writes in the first person, drawing the reader into his solitude and uncertainty. We feel his anxiety, his resolve, his relief. This makes the book not only an intellectual masterpiece, but a spiritual one—a map of the soul's journey from confusion to clarity.

Many of Descartes' conclusions—particularly his dualism, the idea that mind and body are separate substances—would later be challenged and revised. Yet the force of his method, and the power of his question—*What can I know for certain?*—continues to haunt and inspire readers to this day. For anyone who has ever doubted their beliefs, questioned the nature of reality, or sought a stable foundation in a shifting world, *The Meditations* remains a lighthouse in the fog of uncertainty.

READING DESCARTES TODAY: RELEVANCE, CHALLENGES, AND INSIGHT

Why read Descartes in the twenty-first century? Because the problems he faced have not gone away—they've only grown more urgent. In an age of misinformation, fake news, manipulated perception, and deep ideological division, the question of *what we can really know* is more important than ever. Descartes' call to clarity, discipline, and rigorous thinking is an antidote to intellectual laziness and superficial certainty.

Moreover, Descartes speaks directly to our experience of interiority. In a world of external stimulation, social media, and constant distraction, his meditations invite us to return to the inner life—to reflect, to examine, to doubt, and to rebuild. He reminds us that true knowledge does not begin with data, but with introspection.

There are, of course, challenges to reading *The Meditations*. Descartes' prose, especially in translation, can appear dense or overly formal. His arguments sometimes rely on assumptions that modern science has left behind. And his proof of God's existence, while historically significant, may not persuade contemporary readers. But to dismiss Descartes on these grounds is to miss the deeper point: he is not handing down dogma—he is modeling a method.

Read *The Meditations* not as a finished doctrine, but as an exercise in philosophical awakening. Let it unsettle you. Let it provoke you. Let it sharpen your awareness of how you think, what you assume, and why you believe what you believe.

To help with this, read slowly. Read actively. Take notes. Rephrase his arguments in your own words. Engage with his questions: *Could I be dreaming? Could I be deceived?* What must be true if anything is true? And pay attention to the rhythm of the meditations—not just their content, but their tone, their mood, their movement from despair to discovery.

Also, consider how Descartes has shaped the world you live in. His influence extends far beyond philosophy. In science, he pioneered a mechanistic view of nature that helped make modern physics and biology possible. In psychology, his emphasis on consciousness laid the groundwork for later theories of the mind. In ethics and politics, his rational individualism helped inspire Enlightenment ideals of liberty and autonomy.

But perhaps his most enduring legacy is the idea that we *can start over*. That we can question everything, strip away illusion, and find a path to truth—not by relying on others, but by thinking clearly for ourselves. That is the promise of Descartes. That is the challenge he offers every reader.

As you begin your journey through *Meditations on First Philosophy*, remember that you are not simply reading a book—you are participating in an experiment. You are entering a dialogue across centuries with one of history's boldest minds. You are following the footsteps of reason into the depths of doubt and toward the light of understanding.

So set aside distraction. Set aside preconceptions. Take up the method. Ask the questions. And trust that, as Descartes shows us, the way to truth lies not in what we believe, but in how we think.

Welcome to *Meditations of Descartes*. Let this be the beginning of your own philosophy.

MEDITATION I

ON THINGS DOUBTFUL.

Some years ago I realized how many false beliefs I had accepted as truths during my younger years, and how questionable those things were that I had built upon them; and therefore I thought it necessary (if I intended to establish anything that would prove solid and lasting in the sciences) that once in my lifetime I should completely set aside all my previous opinions, and start fresh from some fundamental principles. But this seemed like an enormous undertaking, and I kept waiting for that maturity of years, than which none could be better suited for learning; for this reason I delayed so long, that eventually I would deserve blame if I spent in deliberation the time that remained only for action.

Today I deliberately freed my mind from all worries, secured for myself a time of peace and freedom from all business, and withdrew into solitude; now at last I will freely and earnestly dedicate myself to the complete destruction of all my previous beliefs.

To accomplish this, it won't be necessary for me to prove all of them false (since I may never achieve that). However, because my reason convinces me that I must withhold my agreement from opinions that don't seem completely certain and beyond doubt just as much as I would from those that are clearly false, it will be enough if I reject all those in which I find any reason for doubt.

Neither is it necessary to accomplish this by examining each belief individually (which would be an endless task), but since once the foundation is undermined, whatever is built upon it will naturally collapse on its own, I will therefore directly attack the very principle upon which everything I have believed was based. Namely.

Whatever I have previously accepted as completely true, I received either from my senses or through my senses; but I have frequently discovered that these senses deceive me, and it is wise never to place complete trust in those things that have deceived us, even if only once.

Doubt. But although the senses sometimes deceive us when dealing with distant or tiny objects, there are many other things we cannot doubt even though we know them only through our senses. For instance, that right now I am in this place, that I am sitting by a fire, that I am wearing a winter coat, that I feel this paper with my hands. How can it be denied that these hands or this body belongs to me? Unless I should compare myself to those insane people whose minds are disturbed by such disordered melancholic vapors that they constantly claim to be kings though they are very poor, or imagine themselves dressed in purple robes though they are naked, or believe their heads are made of clay like a bottle, or of glass, and so on. But these are insane people, and I would be just as insane as they are if I followed their example by imagining these things as they do.

Solution. This would indeed seem very clear to those who never sleep, and experience the same things (and sometimes even more improbable events) during their rest, just as these mad people do while they are awake; for how often am I convinced in a dream of these ordinary experiences, that I am in this place, that I am wearing a gown, that I am sitting by a fire, and so on. Though all the while I am lying naked between the sheets.

But now I'm certain that I'm awake and looking at this paper, and this head that I'm shaking isn't asleep. I consciously and deliberately extend this hand, and I can sense that such clear experiences couldn't happen to someone who's sleeping. Yet I can remember being fooled before in my sleep by similar thoughts. When I think about this more carefully, I become so convinced of how difficult it is to tell the difference between sleeping and being awake that I'm astonished, and this very astonishment almost convinces me that I must be asleep.

Doubt. Let us therefore imagine ourselves asleep, and that these things are not real—that we open our eyes, move our heads, stretch out our hands, and perhaps that we have no such things as hands or a body at all. Yet we must acknowledge that what we see in a dream is like a painted picture, which cannot be created except in the likeness of something real; and that therefore these general things at least—eyes, head, hands, and the whole body—are things that truly exist and are not imaginary. For painters themselves, even when they design mermaids and satyrs in the most unusual forms, do not give them completely new natures, but only combine various parts of different animals together. And if by chance they invent something so new that nothing like it has ever been seen, so that it is entirely fictional and false, yet the colors at least from which they create it must be real colors. So in the same way, though these general things like eyes, head, hands, and so forth may be imaginary, we must nevertheless necessarily acknowledge that the simpler and more universal things are true, from which (as from true colors) these images of things in our minds are formed, whether they are true or false. Such things include the nature of a body in general and its extension, also the shape of extended things, along with their quantity or size, their number as well, and the place where they exist, the time in which they endure, and similar things. Therefore we can reasonably conclude from this that physics, both natural and medical, astronomy, and all other sciences that depend on the study of compound things are doubtful. But arithmetic, geometry, and similar disciplines (which deal only with the most simple and general things, not concerning themselves with whether these things really exist or not) contain something certain and undoubted. For whether I sleep or am awake, two and three added together make five;

a square has no more than four sides, and so forth. Nor does it seem possible that such clear truths could be doubted.

Solution. But all this time there remains deeply rooted in my mind a certain long-held belief in the existence of an all-powerful God, by whom I was created in my current state; and how do I know that he didn't cause there to be no Earth, no Heaven, no physical body, no shape, no size, no place, and yet make all these things appear to me exactly as they do now? And just as I frequently observe others making mistakes about things they believe they completely understand, so why couldn't I be deceived whenever I add two and three, or count the sides of a square, or think about any other simple matter?

Doubt. But perhaps God doesn't want me to be deceived, since he is said to be infinitely good.

Solution. Yet if it were contrary to his goodness to create me so that I should always be deceived, it also seems inconsistent with his goodness to permit me to be deceived at any time; though no one will affirm this latter point. There are indeed some who would rather deny God's omnipotence than believe all things are uncertain; but we need not challenge them at present. And we will assume all this about God to be false; yet whether they suppose me to have become what I am through fate, through chance, through a continuous chain of causes, or in any other way, since making errors is an imperfection, the less power they assign to the author of my being, the more probable it becomes that I am so imperfect as to always be deceived.

I don't know how to respond to these arguments and am compelled to admit that there is nothing among all those things I previously accepted as truths that I cannot now doubt; and this doubt will not be based on carelessness or frivolity, but on strong and carefully considered reasons; and therefore I must from now on (if I intend to discover any truths) withhold my agreement from them just as much as from obvious falsehoods.

But it's not enough to think about these things only briefly; I must make sure to remember them. Every day my old opinions return to me and, very much against my will, almost take possession of my belief, tied to them as if by constant habit and the right of familiarity. I will never stop agreeing with and trusting in them as long as I think of them as they really are in themselves—that is to say, somewhat doubtful (as I have now proven), yet nevertheless highly probable, which makes it much more reasonable to believe them than to disbelieve them.

Therefore, I believe I wouldn't be making a mistake if I deliberately turned my mind in the opposite direction and deceived myself by assuming these beliefs are completely false and imaginary for a time. This way, when the weight of prejudice becomes equal on both sides, no bad habit will pull my judgment away from the true understanding of things. I know that no dangerous error will result from this approach, and I cannot be too generous in indulging my own skepticism, since what I'm doing here concerns speculation rather than practice.

To achieve this goal, I will assume that instead of an infinitely perfect God who is the source of truth, there exists some evil spirit that is extremely powerful and cunning, and has used every effort to deceive me. I will imagine that the heavens, air, earth, colors, shapes, sounds, and all external things are nothing more than illusions from dreams, which this spirit has used as traps to ensnare my gullible belief. I will regard myself as having no hands, eyes, flesh, blood, or senses, but as falsely believing that I possess all of these things. I will persist steadfastly in this meditation, and although it may not be within my power to uncover any truth, it is within my power to refuse to accept falsehoods, and with firm determination ensure that this mighty deceiver, no matter how powerful or clever, cannot impose anything upon my belief.

But this is a demanding task, and a certain laziness pulls me back to my ordinary way of life, and like a prisoner who in his sleep perhaps enjoyed an imaginary freedom, and when he begins to suspect that he is dreaming is afraid to wake up, but is willing to be deceived by the pleasant illusion; so I willingly fall back into my old beliefs, and am afraid to be awakened, lest a difficult waking following a pleasant rest I may hereafter live not in the light, but in the confused darkness of the doubts now raised.

MEDITATION II

ON THE NATURE OF THE HUMAN MIND, AND THAT IT IS EASIER TO PROVE ITS EXISTENCE THAN THAT OF OUR BODY.

Through yesterday's meditation, I have been thrown into such profound doubts that I will never be able to forget them, and yet I do not know how to resolve them. Having been suddenly plunged into a deep abyss, I am so overwhelmed that I can neither reach the bottom nor swim to the surface.

Nevertheless, I will try once more, and follow the path I started yesterday, by removing from myself whatever is even slightly doubtful, as if I had definitely discovered it to be completely false, and will continue until I find some certainty, or if nothing else, at least this certainty: that there is nothing certain.

Archimedes needed only a single fixed and immovable point to move the entire Earth, so in this perfect endeavor great achievements can be anticipated if I can find even the smallest thing that is true and beyond dispute.

Therefore, I assume that everything I see is false, and I believe that none of those things actually exist that my unreliable memory presents to me; it's clear I have no senses, that Body, Shape, Extension, Movement, Location, and so on are mere illusions; what then is there that is true? perhaps only this: That nothing is certain.

But how do I know that there is nothing distinct from all these things I have just considered that I have no reason to doubt? Is there no God, or whatever other name I might call him, who has placed these thoughts in my mind? Yet why should I think this? Perhaps I myself am the author of them. On this account, therefore, must I not be something? It was just now that I denied that I had any senses or any body. Wait a moment—am I so bound to a body and senses that I cannot exist without them? But I have convinced myself that there is nothing in the world, no heaven, no earth, no souls, no bodies; and then why not that I myself do not exist? Yet surely if I could convince myself of anything, I existed.

But there is some kind of deceiver, very powerful and very cunning, who constantly tries to deceive me; without doubt therefore I exist, if he can deceive me; And let him deceive me as much as he can, yet he can never make me cease to exist, while I think that I am. Therefore I may establish this as a principle, that whenever this statement I am, I exist, is spoken or thought by me, it is necessarily true.

But I don't yet fully understand who I am as someone who necessarily exists, and I must be careful from now on not to foolishly mistake something else for myself, which would deceive me regarding this thought that I defend as the most certain and evident of all.

Therefore, I will once again recall what I believed myself to be before, prior to beginning these Meditations, and from this understanding I will remove whatever can be disproven by the previously mentioned reasons, so that in the end, only what is true and indisputable may remain.

What have I considered myself to be up until now? A human being. But what exactly is a human being? Should I say a rational animal? Absolutely not, because then someone might ask what an animal is, and what rational means. This way, one question could lead me into even greater complications. Right now, I don't have enough time to waste on such detailed distinctions.

But instead, I'll focus on what previously came to my mind freely and naturally whenever I tried to understand what I myself was.

And the first thing I notice presenting itself is that I have a face, hands, arms, and this entire structure of parts that can be seen in my body, which I call my body.

The next thing that occurred to me was that I was nourished, could walk, had senses, and could think; I attributed these functions to my soul. Yet I did not fully understand what this soul of mine was; or else I imagined it as something small like wind, or fire, or air, flowing through my more solid parts.

As for my body, I truly had no doubt that I correctly understood its nature, which (if I were to try to describe it as I conceive it) I would explain in this way: By a body I mean anything that has shape, or can be contained in a place, and fills a space in such a way that it excludes all other bodies from that same space, something that can be touched, seen, heard, tasted, or smelled, and something that is capable of various movements and changes, not by itself, but through some other thing that moves it, for I considered it contrary to (or rather beyond) the nature of a body to move itself, or to perceive, or to think. Instead, I was amazed that I should find these operations in certain bodies.

But how can I now affirm that I possess any of those things which I have just said belong to the nature of a body, given that I assume there exists a certain powerful and (if it is permissible to call him so) evil deceiver who uses all his efforts to mislead me in everything? Wait—let me consider—let me think—let me reflect—I can find no answer, and I am tired of repeating the same things over and over again in vain.

But which of these abilities did I assign to my soul—my capacity for nutrition or movement? Now that I see I have no body, these are nothing but illusions. Was it my ability to sense things? But this also cannot function without a body, and I seemed to perceive many things while sleeping that I later realized I had not actually sensed. Was it my ability to think? Here I have found it—it is my thought. This alone cannot be separated from me. I am, I exist—this is certain, but for how long do I exist? I exist for as long as I think, because it may be that when I stop thinking, I cease to exist. Now I accept nothing except what is necessarily true: therefore, I am simply a thinking being—that is to say, a mind, a soul, an understanding, or reason—words whose meaning I did not grasp before. I am a real thing that truly exists. But what kind of thing am I? I have just stated it: a thinking thing.

But am I nothing else? I will think about this—I am not that structure of parts called a human body, nor am I any kind of thin air flowing through those parts, nor wind, nor fire, nor vapor, nor breath, nor anything else I can imagine, because I have assumed all these things do not exist. Yet my position remains solid; I am still something. But perhaps it happens that these very things I assume don't exist (because they are unknown to me) are actually no different from that very self which I know. I cannot say for certain, I won't argue about it now, I can only give my opinion about those things I have some knowledge of. I am certain that I exist, I ask who I am that I know in this way, certainly, the knowledge of myself (precisely understood) does not depend on those things whose existence I am still unaware of; and therefore not on any other things that I can create through my imagination.

And this very word "feign" reminds me of my mistake, because I would indeed be pretending if I imagined myself to be anything physical; since imagining is simply thinking about the shape or form of a material object. But now I know with certainty that I exist, and I also know that it's possible that all these mental images, and everything that relates to physical nature in general, are nothing more than misleading illusions. When I consider these facts, it would be just as foolish for me to say "I will use my imagination to better understand what I am" as it would be to say "Right now I'm awake and I perceive something real, but since it's not clear enough, I'll try to fall asleep so I can perceive it more clearly and accurately in a dream."

Therefore, I understand that nothing I can grasp through my imagination can be part of my understanding of myself, and I must carefully pull my mind away from those things so that it can more clearly perceive its own nature.

Let me ask therefore: What am I? A thinking being, but what is that? That is something that doubts, understands, affirms, denies, wills, refuses, imagines, and perceives. These are truly not just a few characteristics, if they all belong to me. And why should they not belong to me? For am I not the very same person who currently doubts almost everything, yet understands something, which I alone affirm to be true, I deny all other things, I want to know more, I would not want to be deceived, I imagine many things against my will, and consider many things as coming to me through my senses. Which of all these abilities is not as true as the fact that I exist, even if I were sleeping, or even if my Creator were doing everything in his power to deceive me? Which of them is distinct from my thought? Which of them

18

can be separated from me? For the fact that I am the same person who doubts, understands, and wills is so clear that I don't know how to explain it more obviously, and that I am also the same person who imagines, for although perhaps (as I have assumed) nothing that can be imagined is true, yet the power of imagination itself really exists and forms part of my thought; and finally that I am the same person who perceives, or notices physical things as if through my senses, yet that I now see light, hear a sound, feel heat, these things are false, for I assume I am asleep, but I know that I see, hear, and feel warmth, and that cannot be false; and this is what in me is properly called sensation, and this strictly understood is the same as thought.

Through these reflections, I'm starting to get a somewhat better grasp of who I am and what I consist of. However, it still appears to me—and I can't help but feel— that physical objects, whose mental images form in my mind and which I perceive through my senses, are understood far more clearly than that vague concept I have of myself, which my imagination fails to provide me with any clear picture of. Yet it's peculiar that things which are uncertain, unfamiliar, and separate from me should be grasped more clearly by me than something that is real, something that is known, or than myself. The reason for this is that my mind tends to drift and wander, refusing to confine itself within the precise boundaries of truth.

Let it wander freely, then, and once more let me give it complete freedom, so that afterward, when properly restrained, it may allow itself to be more easily controlled.

Let me think about those things that I used to believe were the most obvious of all things—namely, physical objects that we can touch and see. I'm not talking about bodies in general, since those broad concepts tend to be unclear, but rather some specific individual body.

Let us choose, for example, this piece of beeswax. It was recently taken from the comb, it has not yet lost all the taste of the honey, it retains something of the smell of the flowers from which it was gathered, its color, shape, and size are evident, it is hard, it is cold, it is easily felt, and if you knock it with your finger, it will make a noise. In short, it has all things necessary for the most perfect understanding of a body.

But look, while I'm speaking, the wax is placed in the fire. Its taste disappears, the smell vanishes, the color changes, the shape transforms, its size increases, it becomes soft, it grows hot, it can barely be touched, and now (even if you strike it) it makes no sound. Does it still remain the same wax? Certainly it does—everyone agrees with this, no one denies it, no one questions it. What then was there in it that was so clearly known? Surely none of those things which I perceived through my senses; for everything I smelled, tasted, saw, felt, or heard has vanished, and yet the wax remains. Perhaps it was only this that I now think about: that the wax itself was not that taste of honey, that smell of flowers, that whiteness, that shape, or that sound, but it was a substance which appeared to me modified in one way before, but now appears differently. But what exactly is it that I imagine in this way? Let me think about this: After rejecting everything that doesn't belong to the wax, let me see what remains—namely, only this: something extended, flexible, and changeable. But what does flexible and changeable mean? Is it that I imagine this wax can be transformed from round to square, or from square to triangular? No, that's not it; for I understand it to be capable of countless such changes, and yet I cannot run through these countless possibilities with my imagination. Therefore, this concept of its changeability doesn't come from my imagination. What then is extended? Isn't its extension also unknown? For when it melts it becomes larger, when it boils it becomes even larger, and larger still when the heat increases; and I wouldn't judge the wax correctly if I didn't think it capable of more varied extensions than I can imagine. It remains for me only to admit that I cannot imagine what this wax is, but that I understand with my mind what it is. I speak of this particular piece of wax, for the concept of wax in general is clearer.

But what is this wax that I understand only through my mind? It is the same wax that I see, that I touch, that I imagine, and ultimately, the same wax that I initially believed it to be. However, it should be noted that my perception of it is not sight, touch, or imagination; nor was it ever these things, even though it initially appeared to be so. Rather, my perception of it is purely an examination or observation of the mind alone, which can be either imperfect and confused, as it was before, or clear and distinct, as it is now, depending on how thoroughly I examine the nature of the wax.

In the meantime, I can't help but notice how easily my mind falls into error; even though I think through these ideas quietly to myself without speaking aloud, I still get caught up in mere words and am nearly misled by our ordinary ways of talking. We typically say that we see the wax itself when it's in front of us, rather than saying we judge it to be present based on its color or shape. From this, I might immediately conclude that wax is known through sight alone, not through mental examination. I would have reached this conclusion if I hadn't happened to look out my window and observe people walking by on the street. I say I see these people just as naturally as I now say I see this wax, yet I actually see nothing more than their hair and clothing, which might only be covering mechanical devices and movements. Instead, I judge them to be human beings. So what I believed I was simply seeing with my eyes, I actually understand through my faculty of judgment, which is my mind. However, someone who wants to think more clearly than ordinary people shouldn't let these common expressions, which ordinary people have created, become sources of confusion.

Therefore, let us move forward and examine whether I understood more clearly and obviously what the wax was when I first looked at it and believed I knew it through my external senses, or at least through my common sense (as it is called), that is to say, through my imagination; or whether I now have a better understanding of it, after I have more carefully investigated both what it is and how it can be known. Certainly it would be foolish to question which of these approaches is true; What was there in my first perception that was clear? What was there that did not seem common to every other animal? But now when I separate the wax from its external qualities and consider it as if it were bare, with its coverings stripped away, then I cannot help but truly perceive it with my mind, though my judgment may still be in error.

But what should I say now about my mind, or myself? (since I still acknowledge nothing as belonging to me except a mind.) Why shouldn't I, who seem to perceive this wax so clearly, know myself not only more truly and more certainly, but also more clearly and obviously? If I conclude that this wax exists because I see it, then it will certainly be much more obvious that I myself exist because I see this wax. It's possible that what I see isn't really wax, and it's also possible that I don't have eyes to see anything with. But it's impossible that when I see, or (which amounts to the same thing) when I think I see, that I who think should not exist. The same reasoning applies if I conclude that this wax exists because I touch it, or imagine it, and so on. What I've said about wax can be applied to all other external things.

Furthermore, if my understanding of wax becomes clearer after I learn about it not just through sight or touch, but through many other means as well, then I must acknowledge that I know myself even more clearly. This is because every type of reasoning that helps me understand wax, or any other physical object, also strengthens the evidence for understanding my own mind. However, there are so many additional aspects within the mind itself that can make my understanding of it more precise, that the things we learn from physical objects barely deserve mention when it comes to knowing the mind.

And now I find myself exactly where I wanted to be; having discovered that physical objects are not truly perceived through our senses or imagination, but only through our understanding, and are not perceived simply because we touch or see them, but because we comprehend them; it becomes clear to me that nothing can possibly be perceived more easily or more clearly than my own mind.

But since I cannot quickly abandon the familiarity of my previous beliefs, I am willing to pause here, so that this new understanding may become more firmly established in my memory through extended reflection.

MEDITATION III.

OF GOD, AND THAT THERE IS A GOD.

Now I will close my eyes, stop my ears, and withdraw all my senses. I will erase the images of physical things completely from my mind, or since that can hardly be achieved, I will pay no attention to them, treating them as empty and false. By talking with myself and examining my own nature more carefully, I will try to make myself gradually more known and familiar to myself.

I am a thinking being, which means I doubt, affirm, deny, understand a few things, remain ignorant of many things, will, refuse to will, imagine, and perceive through my senses. For as I noted earlier, although perhaps whatever I imagine or sense as existing outside of me may not actually exist, I am certain that those ways of thinking which I call sensation and imagination (since they are simply particular modes of thinking) do exist within me. So in these few words I have mentioned everything I know, or at least everything I currently perceive myself to know.

Now I will examine myself more carefully to see whether there might be something else within me that I have not yet noticed. I am certain that I am a thinking being, so don't I know what is required to be sure of anything? My answer is that in this first knowledge of mine, there is nothing but a clear and distinct perception of what I affirm, which would not be enough to make me certain of the truth of something if it were possible that anything I perceive so clearly and distinctly could be false. Therefore, I can establish this as a principle: Whatever I clearly and distinctly perceive is certainly true.

But I have previously accepted many things as absolutely certain and obvious, which I later discovered to be questionable. So what kinds of things were these? Namely, the heavens, the earth, the stars, and all other objects that I experienced through my senses. But what did I clearly perceive about these things? Simply that I had ideas or thoughts of these objects in my mind, and I cannot deny at present that I possess these ideas within me. However, there was something else that I asserted, and which (due to the ordinary way of believing) I thought I clearly perceived; yet in reality, I did not truly perceive it. This was the notion that certain things existed outside of me from which these ideas originated, and to which they bore exact resemblance. And it was in this matter that I was either mistaken, or if I happened to judge correctly, it did not result from the power of my perception.

But when I was working through any simple and easy proposition in arithmetic or geometry, such as that two and three added together make five, didn't I perceive them clearly enough to make me affirm them as true? Truly concerning these I had no other reason afterwards to doubt, except that I thought perhaps there may be a God who might have created me in such a way that I should be deceived even in those things which seemed most clear to me. And as often as this preconceived opinion of God's great power comes into my mind, I cannot help but confess that he may easily cause me to err even in those things which I think I perceive most evidently with my mind; yet as often as I consider the things themselves, which I judge myself to perceive so clearly, I am so fully persuaded by them, that I easily break out into these expressions: Let whoever can deceive me, yet he shall never cause me not to be while I think that I am, or that it shall ever be true that I never was, while at present it is true that I am, or perhaps, that two and three added together make more or less than five; for in these things I perceive a manifest contradiction. And truly seeing I have no reason to think any God a deceiver, nor as yet fully know whether there is any God or not, it is but a slight and (as I may say) metaphysical reason of doubt, which depends only on that opinion of which I am not yet persuaded.

Therefore, to remove this obstacle, when I have time I should investigate whether God exists, and if He does exist, whether He can be a deceiver. For as long as I remain ignorant of this, I cannot possibly be completely certain of anything else.

But now method seems to require me to organize all my thoughts under certain categories, and to examine which of them properly contains truth or falsehood. Some of them are like images of things, and to these alone the name of an idea properly belongs, such as when I think about a man, a chimera or monster, heaven, an angel, or God. But there are others that have additional forms added to them, such as when I will, when I fear, when I affirm, when I deny. I know I always have some particular thing as the subject or object of my thought whenever I think, but in this last type of thoughts there is something more that I think about than merely the likeness of the thing. And of these thoughts some are called wills and emotions, and others are called judgments.

Now regarding ideas, if they are considered alone as they exist in themselves, without reference to any other things, they cannot properly be false; for whether I imagine a goat or a chimera, it is as certain that I imagine one as the other. Also in the will and emotions I need not fear any falsehood, for though I should wish for evil things, or things that do not exist, it is not therefore untrue that I wish for them.

Therefore, only my judgments about things remain, and I must be careful not to be deceived in them. Now the main and most common error I find in these judgments is that I assume the ideas within me correspond to and resemble certain things outside of me; for truly, if I consider these ideas simply as particular modes of my thinking, without reference to anything else, they would hardly give me any reason to make mistakes.

Of these ideas, some are innate, some are adventitious, and others seem to me to be created by myself. For my understanding of what a thing is, what truth is, and what a thought is appears to come purely from my own nature. But when I hear a noise, see the sun, or feel heat, I have always judged these to come from external things. Finally, mermaids, griffins, and similar monsters are created entirely by myself. Yet I might well consider all of them to be either adventitious, or all of them innate, or all of them made by myself, since I have not yet discovered their true origin.

But I should mainly focus on examining those ideas that I consider to be adventitious, which I believe come from external objects, so that I can determine what reason I have to think they resemble the actual things they represent. Nature teaches me this; and I also know that these ideas don't depend on my will, and therefore not on me, because they often appear to me against my preferences, or as people say, against my will. For instance, right now, whether I want to or not, I feel heat, and therefore I believe that this sensation or idea of heat is transmitted to me by something truly separate from myself, namely by the heat of the fire beside which I'm sitting. Nothing seems more natural than for me to conclude that this thing should send its own likeness to me, rather than having something else transmitted by it. I will now test whether this type of reasoning is sound enough or not.

When I say here that nature teaches me this, I mean only that I am compelled to believe it almost involuntarily, not that it is revealed to me as true through any natural light; these two things are very different. Whatever is revealed to me by the light of nature (such as the fact that I necessarily exist because I think) cannot possibly be doubted, because I possess no other faculty in which I can place such great confidence as I can in the light of nature, nor any faculty that could possibly tell me that those things are false which the natural light teaches me are true. As for my natural inclinations, I have often found in the past that they have led me to choose the worse option when I was deciding between two good things, and therefore I see no reason why I should trust them in any other matter.

And then, although these ideas don't depend on my will, it doesn't necessarily follow that they must come from external things. For just as those inclinations I just mentioned are within me, yet they seem separate and different from my will, so perhaps there may be some other faculty in me that I'm unaware of, which could be the actual cause of these ideas. After all, I've noticed that ideas are formed in me while I dream, without any help from external objects.

And finally, even if these ideas come from things that are different from me, it doesn't necessarily mean they must resemble those things. I have often discovered that the actual thing and my idea of it differ greatly. For instance, I have two different ideas of the Sun within myself: one that

I receive through my senses (which I primarily classify among what I call adventitious ideas), through which the Sun appears very small to me, and another that comes from astronomical reasoning (that is, logically derived or otherwise formed by me from certain natural concepts), through which the Sun appears larger than the Earth itself. Clearly, both of these ideas cannot be like the actual Sun that exists outside of me, and my reason convinces me that the idea which seems to come directly from the Sun itself is actually the least like the real Sun.*

Everything I've described clearly demonstrates that up until now, I haven't been making decisions based on sound reasoning, but rather acting on blind impulse when I believed that certain things exist separately from myself, and that these things have transmitted their ideas or images to me through my sensory organs or through some other means.

But I have another way of investigating whether any of those things whose ideas I have within me actually exist outside of me. Here's how it works: Since these ideas are simply modes of thinking, I recognize no inequality between them, and they all come from me in the same way. However, since one represents one thing and another represents something different, there's clearly a great difference between them. Without a doubt, those ideas that represent substances contain something more, or as I might put it, have more objective reality in them than those that represent only modes or accidents. Furthermore, the idea through which I understand a supreme God—eternal, infinite, all-knowing, all-powerful, and creator of all things besides himself—certainly contains more objective reality than those ideas through which finite substances are presented.*

But now, it's clear from natural reasoning that there must be at least as much in the complete efficient cause as there is in the effect of that cause. Where else could the effect get its reality except from the cause? And how could the cause give it that reality unless it possessed that reality itself?

And from this it follows that nothing can be created from nothing, nor can something that is more perfect (that is, which contains more reality within itself) come from something that is less perfect.

And this is clearly true, not only in those effects whose actual or formal reality is considered, but in those ideas also, whose objective reality is only respected; that is to say, for example of illustration, it is not only impossible that a stone, which was not, should now begin to be, unless it were produced by something, in which, whatever goes to the making a stone, is either formally or virtually; neither can heat be produced in any thing, which before was not hot, but by a thing which is at least of as equal a degree of perfection as heat is; but also it is impossible that I should have an idea of heat, or of a stone, unless it were put into me by some cause, in which there is at least as much reality, as I conceive there is in heat or a stone. For though that cause transfers none of its own actual or formal reality into my idea, I must not from thence conclude that it is less real; but I may think that the nature of the idea itself is such, that of itself it requires no other formal reality, but what it has from my thought, of which it is a mode. But that this idea has this or that objective reality, rather than any other, proceeds clearly from some cause, in which there ought to be at least as much formal reality, as there is of objective reality in the idea itself. For if we suppose anything in the idea, which was not in its cause, it must of necessity have this from nothing; but though it be a most imperfect manner of existing, by which the thing is objectively in the intellect by an idea, yet it is not altogether nothing, and therefore cannot proceed from nothing.

I shouldn't doubt that the reality I perceive in my ideas is merely objective reality, and therefore conclude that the same reality must necessarily exist formally in the causes of these ideas. However, I may conclude that it's sufficient for this reality to exist only objectively in those very causes. Just as that objective manner of being belongs to the very nature of an idea, so that formal manner of being belongs to the very nature of a cause of ideas, at least to the first and most important causes of them. Although perhaps one idea may derive from another, we cannot proceed infinitely, but must eventually arrive at some first idea, whose cause is like an original copy, in which all the objective reality of the idea is formally contained. Thus I clearly discover by the light of nature that the ideas which are in me are like pictures, which may easily fall short of the perfection of those things from which they are taken, but cannot contain anything greater or more perfect than them. The longer and more carefully I examine these things, the more clearly and distinctly I discover them to be true.

But what should I conclude from this? Simply this: if the objective reality of any of my ideas is such that it cannot exist in me either formally or eminently, and therefore I cannot be the cause of that idea, it necessarily follows that not only do I exist alone, but that some other thing, which is the cause of that idea, must also exist.

But if I cannot find such an idea within me, I have no argument to convince me that anything else exists besides myself, for I have carefully searched, and so far I have been unable to discover any other convincing evidence.

Some of these ideas exist (in addition to the one that represents myself to myself, which I cannot doubt in this instance) that represent to me various things: one represents God, others represent physical and lifeless objects, some represent angels, others represent animals, and finally some represent people like myself.

Regarding those ideas that represent people, angels, or animals, I can easily understand that they might be composed of the ideas I have of myself, of physical things, and of God, even if there were no other people besides myself, no angels, and no animals in existence.

When it comes to the ideas of physical things, I find nothing in them that suggests such perfection that it couldn't come from myself. When I examine them more closely and investigate them more thoroughly, just as I did yesterday in the second meditation with the idea of wax, I discover that there are only a few things I perceive clearly and distinctly in them. These include magnitude or extension in length, width, and depth; the figure or shape that results from the boundaries of that extension; the position or location that various shaped bodies have in relation to each other; and their motion or change of location. To these we can add their substance, duration, and number. As for the others, such as light, colors, sounds, smells, tastes, heat, and cold, along with other tactile qualities, I have only very unclear and confused thoughts about them. I don't know whether they are true or false—that is, whether the ideas I have of them are ideas of things that actually exist or don't exist.

Although falsehood, formally and properly speaking, exists only in judgment (as I noted before), there is another kind of material falsehood in ideas when they represent something as actually existing even though it doesn't exist.

For instance, the ideas I have of heat and cold are so unclear and confused that I can't determine from them whether cold is simply the absence of heat, or heat is the absence of cold, or whether either of them is a real quality, or whether neither of them is real. Since every idea must resemble the thing it represents, if it's true that cold is nothing but the absence of heat, then the idea that represents cold to me as something real and positive deserves to be called false. The same principle can be applied to other ideas.

And now I see no reason why I should assign any other source of these ideas but myself; for if they are false, that is, represent things that do not exist, I know by natural understanding that they come from nothing; that is to say, I hold them for no other reason than because my nature lacks something and is imperfect. But if they are true, yet since I find so little reality in them that this very reality hardly seems to be real, I see no reason why I myself should not be their source.

But some of those very clear and distinct ideas of physical things also seem to have been borrowed from the idea I have of myself, such as substance, duration, number, and similar concepts. When I think of a stone as a substance (meaning something capable of existing on its own) and also think of myself as a substance, even though I understand myself to be a thinking substance that isn't extended in space, while the stone is an extended substance that doesn't think—creating a significant difference between these two concepts—they still share the common feature of both being substances. Similarly, when I think of myself as existing now and remember that I existed before, and since I have various thoughts that I can count, this is how I acquire the concepts of duration and number, which I then apply to other things.

Regarding those other qualities that make up the concept of a physical body—such as extension, shape, location, and movement—these are not actually present in me in their literal form, since I am merely a thinking being. However, because these are simply different modes or ways that substance can exist, and since I myself am also a substance, it appears that these qualities could exist within me in a higher or more perfect form.

*Therefore, only the idea of God remains, and I must examine whether it contains something that could not possibly have originated from me. By the word God, I mean a certain infinite substance, independent, all-knowing, all-powerful, by whom both I myself and everything else that exists (if anything actually exists) was created. All these attributes are of such an elevated nature that the more carefully I consider them, the less I can conceive of myself as possibly being the author of these concepts.

From what has been said, I must conclude that God exists. While the idea of substance can arise in me because I myself am a substance, I could not have the idea of an infinite substance (since I myself am finite) unless it came from a substance that is truly infinite. I should not think that I have no genuine idea of infinity, or that I perceive it only through the negation of what is finite, the way I understand rest and darkness through the negation or absence of motion or light. On the contrary, I clearly understand that there is more reality in an infinite substance than in a finite one, and therefore my perception of the infinite (as God) comes before my notion of the finite (as myself). How could I know that I doubt or desire—that is, that I lack something and am not completely perfect—unless I had the idea of a being more perfect than myself, by comparing myself to which I can discover my own imperfections?

Neither can it be said that this idea of God is materially false, and that it therefore comes from nothing, as I previously observed about the ideas of heat and cold, and so forth. On the contrary, since this concept is extremely clear and distinct, and contains within itself more objective reality than any other idea, none can be more true in itself, nor can any be found in which there is less suspicion of falsehood. This idea of an infinitely perfect being is most true, for although it may be supposed that such a being does not exist, it cannot be supposed that the idea of such a being presents nothing real to me, as I have said before about the idea of cold. This idea is also most clear and distinct, for whatever I perceive clearly and distinctly to be real, true, and perfect, is entirely contained in this idea of God.

No one can argue that I cannot understand the Infinite, or that there are countless other aspects of God that I cannot conceive or even begin to think about; this is simply the nature of the Infinite—it cannot be fully grasped by me, a finite being. It is enough for me to prove that my idea of God is the truest, clearest, and most distinct of all the ideas I possess, based on the fact that I understand God cannot be fully understood, and that I recognize whatever I clearly perceive and know to involve any perfection, along with perhaps countless other perfections I am unaware of, exists in God either formally or eminently.

Doubt. But perhaps I am something more than I take myself to be, and perhaps all these perfections which I attribute to God are potentially in me, though at present they do not show themselves and break into action. For I am now fully experienced that my knowledge may be increased, and I see nothing that prevents why it may not increase by degrees infinitely, nor why through my knowledge so increased I may not attain to the other perfections of God; nor lastly, why the power or aptitude of having these perfections may not be sufficient to produce the idea of them in me.

Solution. But none of these explanations will work; for first, although it is true that my knowledge can be increased, and that many things exist in me potentially which are not yet actual, none of these factors contribute to forming an idea of God, in which I conceive nothing as potential, because it is a clear sign of imperfection that something can be increased gradually. Furthermore, although my knowledge may be increased more and more, I know that it can never become actually infinite, because it can never reach that level of perfection which does not allow for a higher degree. But I conceive God to be actually so infinite that nothing can be added to his perfections. And finally, I perceive that the objective existence of an idea cannot be produced merely by the potential existence of a thing (which, properly speaking, is nothing) but requires an actual or formal existence for its production.

Of all the things I've mentioned, there's nothing that isn't clear through reason to anyone who carefully considers them. However, when I'm not paying attention and images of physical things cloud my understanding, I don't easily remember the reasons why the idea of a being more perfect than myself must necessarily come from a being that is actually more perfect. Therefore, I need to investigate further whether I, who have this idea, could possibly exist unless such a being actually existed. To do this, let me ask: where would I come from? From myself? From my parents? From something else less perfect than God? Nothing can be thought of or imagined as more perfect than God, or even equally perfect with God.

But first, if I came from myself, I wouldn't doubt, desire, or lack anything, because I would have given myself all the perfections I can conceive of, and as a result I myself would be God. I cannot believe that the things I lack are harder to obtain than the things I already possess. On the contrary, it's clear that it would be much more difficult for me (that is, a thinking substance) to emerge from nothing than for me to gain knowledge of the many things I don't understand, which are merely attributes of that substance. And certainly if I had that greater thing (namely, existence) from myself, I wouldn't have denied myself not only those things that might be easier to acquire, but also all those things that I perceive are contained in the idea of God. The reason is that nothing else seems more difficult for me to accomplish, and certainly if they were actually more difficult, they would appear more difficult to me (assuming that whatever I have, I have from myself), because in those matters I would discover the limits of my power.

I cannot escape the force of these arguments by assuming that I have always existed as I am now, and therefore don't need to search for a creator of my existence. The duration or continuance of my life can be divided into countless parts, each of which doesn't depend on the other parts at all. Therefore, it doesn't follow that because I existed a while ago, I must necessarily exist now. This won't follow unless I assume some cause to create me anew for this moment (that is, to preserve me). It's clear to anyone who considers the nature of duration that the same power and action required to preserve something at each moment of its existence is the same as what's needed to create that thing anew if it didn't exist. This is one of those principles that are evident by the light of nature: that the act of preservation differs only in reason (as philosophers call it) from the act of creation.

Therefore, I should ask myself this question: do I, who exist now, have any power to make myself continue to exist in the future? If I had such power, I would certainly be aware of it, since I am nothing but a thinking being, or at least right now I am only considering that part of myself which thinks. To this question, I answer that I cannot find any such power within me. As a result, I clearly understand that I depend on some other being separate from myself.

But what if I argue that perhaps this Being is not God, but that I am created either by my parents, or some other causes less perfect than God? In response to this, let me consider (as I have mentioned before) that it is clear that whatever exists in the effect must at least exist in the cause; and therefore since I am a thinking being, and have within me an idea of God, it necessarily follows that whatever kind of cause I assign to my own existence must also be a thinking being, and must possess an idea of all those perfections which I attribute to God. Concerning this cause, we may again ask whether it exists by itself, or from some other cause. If it exists by itself, it is evident (from what has been stated) that it must be God; for since it has the power to exist by itself, it undoubtedly also has the power to actually possess all those perfections of which it has an idea within itself, that is, all those perfections which I conceive in God. But if it exists from another cause, we may again ask of that cause whether it exists by itself, or from another; until at length we arrive at the ultimate cause of all, which will be God. For it is clear that this inquiry cannot proceed infinitely, especially when at present I am concerned not only with that cause which first created me, but primarily with that which preserves me at this very moment.

Neither can it be assumed that many separate causes have worked together to create me, and that I received the idea of one of God's perfections from one of them, and from another the idea of a different perfection; and that therefore all these perfections are to be found scattered throughout the world, but not all of them united in any one being who could be God. For on the contrary, unity, simplicity, or the inseparability of all God's attributes is one of the chief perfections which I understand in Him; and certainly the idea of the unity of the divine perfections could not be created in me by any other cause than by that from which I have received the ideas of his other perfections; for it is impossible to make me understand these perfections as connected and inseparable, unless he should also make me know what these perfections are.

Finally, regarding my existence coming from my parents. Although whatever thoughts I have previously held about them were true, they certainly contribute nothing to my preservation, nor do I come from them as a thinking being, for they have only prepared that material thing in which I, that is, my mind (which alone I presently consider to be myself) dwells. Therefore I cannot now question that I descended from them. But I must necessarily conclude that because I exist, and because I have an idea of a most perfect Being, that is, of God, it clearly follows that God exists.

Now it only remains for me to examine how I have received this idea of God. I have not received it through my senses, nor does it come to me without my deliberate thought, as the ideas of sensible things usually do when such things act upon the organs of my senses, or at least appear to do so. This idea is not created by myself either, for I can neither take away from it nor add anything to it. Therefore, I can only conclude that it is innate, just as the idea of myself is natural to me.

And truly it is not to be wondered at that God in creating me should imprint this idea in me, so that it may remain there as a stamp impressed by the workman God on me his work, nor is it necessary that this stamp should be a thing different from the work itself, but it is very believable (from this alone that God created me) that I am made as it were according to his likeness and image, and that the same likeness, in which the idea of God is contained, is perceived by me with the same faculty with which I perceive myself; That is to say, while I reflect upon myself, I do not only perceive that I am an imperfect thing, having my dependence upon some other thing, and that I am a thing that desires more and better things indefinitely; But also at the same time I understand that He on whom I depend contains in him all those wished for things (not only indefinitely and potentially, but) actually, indefinitely; and that therefore he is God. The whole force of this argument lies thus, because I know it impossible for me to be of the same nature I am, namely having the idea of a God in me, unless really there were a God, a God (I say) that very same God, whose idea I have in my mind (that is, having all those perfections, which I cannot comprehend, but can as it were think upon them) and who is not subject to any defects.*

From this it's clear that God is not a deceiver, since it's obvious through natural reason that all fraud and deception stems from some kind of flaw or imperfection. But before I continue further with this line of thinking or explore other truths that might follow from it, I want to pause here and focus on contemplating this God, to reflect on His divine qualities, to observe, marvel at, and worship the beauty of this infinite light, as much as my limited understanding allows me to grasp. Just as we believe through faith that the greatest joy of the afterlife consists entirely in contemplating God's divine majesty, we also discover through experience that this contemplation gives us the greatest pleasure we can experience in this present life, even though it remains far more incomplete than what awaits us in the next.

MEDITATION IV.

OF TRUTH AND FALSEHOOD.

Lately, I have become accustomed to withdrawing my mind from my senses, and I have thoroughly considered how few things relating to physical bodies are truly perceived, while there are many more things concerning the human mind, and even more concerning God, that are well known. Now I can easily turn my thoughts from sensible things to those that are purely intelligible and separated from matter. Indeed, I have a much clearer idea of the human mind—as a thinking thing that has no physical dimensions of length, width, and height, nor any other physical qualities—than I could have of any physical thing. When I reflect upon myself and consider that I doubt, meaning I am an imperfect and dependent being, I gather from this a clear and distinct idea of an independent, perfect being, which is God. From the fact alone that I have such an idea—that is, because I who have this idea do myself exist—I conclude so clearly that God also exists, and that my being depends on him every moment, that I am confident nothing can be known more evidently and certainly by human understanding.

And now I seem to see a way by which, through this contemplation of the true God, in whom the treasures of knowledge and wisdom are hidden, I may reach the understanding of other things.

And first, I know it's impossible for God to deceive me. In all cheating and deception, there exists some form of imperfection. Although the ability to deceive might appear to demonstrate cleverness and power, having the desire to deceive is undoubtedly a sign of malice and weakness, and therefore cannot be attributed to God.

I have also discovered within myself a faculty of judgment, which I certainly received from God (like everything else I possess). Since God will not deceive me, he has surely given me such judgment that I can never make an error when I use it correctly. I cannot doubt this truth, unless it appears that it would follow from this that I can therefore never make an error at all. For if everything I have comes from God, and if he gave me no capacity for making errors, it would seem that I cannot make errors. And indeed this is true when I think about God and completely turn my attention to contemplating him—I find no opportunity for error or deception. But when I return to contemplating myself, I discover that I am subject to countless errors. When I investigate the cause of this, I find within myself not only a real and positive idea of God—that is, of a being who is infinitely perfect—but also (if I may put it this way) a negative idea of nothingness. In other words, I am positioned between God and nothingness, or between a perfect being and non-being. As a creation of the Supreme Being, there is nothing in me that could cause me to be deceived or led into error. But insofar as I participate in nothingness, or in non-being—that is, insofar as I myself am not the Supreme Being and lack many perfections—it is no wonder that I should be deceived.

By this I mean that Error (as it is Error) is not any real existence that depends on God, but it is only a deficiency; And that therefore to make me make mistakes there is no need for a faculty of making errors given to me by God, but it simply happens that I make mistakes merely because the faculty of judgment, which he has given me, is not infinite.*

But this explanation still isn't completely satisfying; error isn't just a simple absence of something, but rather a deprivation, or the lack of certain knowledge that should rightfully exist within me. When I reflect on God's nature, it appears impossible that he would grant me any ability that isn't perfect in its own way, or that would be missing any of its proper qualities; because the more skilled an artisan is, the more perfect are the works that come from his hands. What could the Supreme Creator of all things make that isn't completely perfect? I cannot question that God has the power to create me in such a way that I would never be misled, nor can I question that he desires whatever is best; so is it better for me to be deceived, or not to be deceived?

When I think about these matters more carefully, several things come to mind. First, I shouldn't be surprised that God does things I cannot explain, nor should I doubt His existence simply because there are many things He does that I don't understand—neither why nor how they happen. Since I now recognize that my nature is very weak and limited, while God's nature is vast, beyond comprehension, and infinite, I must fully grasp that He can accomplish countless things whose causes remain hidden from me. For this reason alone, I consider all those explanations that are based on purpose (that is, final causes) to be useless in natural philosophy, because I cannot presume to think myself capable of discovering God's plans without being reckless.

I also understand that whenever we try to determine whether God's works are perfect, we shouldn't focus on any single type of creature by itself, but rather on the entire universe of beings. What might rightfully appear imperfect when viewed in isolation could actually be completely perfect as part of the world as a whole. Although I have questioned everything and discovered nothing that certainly exists except myself and God, I cannot deny that since I have contemplated God's omnipotence, many other things are created by him, or at least could be created by him, meaning that I myself might be part of this universe.

Furthermore, looking more closely at myself and examining what these errors of mine actually are (which serve as the only evidence of my imperfection), I discover that they stem from two contributing causes: my ability to know and my ability to choose or the freedom of my will—in other words, from both my understanding and my will working together. Through my understanding alone, I simply perceive ideas upon which I form judgments, and in this process (taken precisely as such) there cannot be any error in the strict sense. Although there may be countless things whose ideas I do not possess within me, I cannot properly be said to be deprived of them, but rather I simply lack them in a negative sense. I cannot demonstrate that God should have granted me a greater capacity for knowledge. And while I recognize him as a masterful creator, I cannot believe that he should have placed all those perfections individually in each of his works that he might have bestowed upon some of them.

I cannot complain that God has not given me a will, or freedom of choice, that is large and perfect enough; for I have experienced that it is not limited by any boundaries.

It's worth noting that I have nothing in me that is so perfect and great, yet I understand that there could be something more perfect and greater. For example, when I consider my ability to understand, I immediately recognize that mine is very small and limited, and at the same time I form an idea of another understanding that is not only much greater, but the greatest and infinite, which I perceive belongs to God. Similarly, when I examine memory or imagination or any other abilities, I find them weak and limited in myself, but in God I understand them to be infinite. There is therefore only my will or freedom of choice, which I find to be so great that I cannot conceive of one greater, so it is primarily through this that I understand myself to bear the likeness and image of God. For although God's will is incomparably greater than mine, both in terms of the knowledge and power that are joined with it, which make it more strong and effective, and also regarding its object, since God can apply himself to more things than I can, yet when considered formally and precisely, God's will seems no greater than mine. For freedom of will consists only in this: that we can do or not do such a thing (that is, affirm or deny, pursue or avoid) or rather only in this: that we are so moved toward a thing that is proposed by our intellect to affirm or deny, pursue or shun, that we are aware that we are not determined to choose it or reject it by any external force.

Neither is it necessary to make someone free that they should have an inclination toward both sides. On the contrary, the more strongly I am inclined toward one side (whether it is because I clearly perceive good or evil in it, or whether it is because God has arranged my inner thoughts in this way), the more free I am in my choice.

Neither God's Grace nor Natural Knowledge truly take away from my liberty, but rather increase and strengthen it. For that indifference which I find in myself, when no reason inclines me more to one side than to the other, is the lowest sort of liberty, and is so far from being a sign of perfection that it only demonstrates a defect or absence of knowledge; for if I should always clearly see what were true and good I should never deliberate in my judgment or choice, and consequently, though I were perfectly free, yet I should never be indifferent.

From all of this, I understand that neither my power of willing, taken exactly as it is, which I have received from God, is the cause of my errors, since it is completely full and perfect in its nature; nor is my power of understanding the cause, because whatever I understand (since it is from God that I understand it) I understand correctly, and I cannot be deceived in this regard.

Where do all my errors come from? I answer that they arise solely from this: since my will extends itself further than my understanding, I don't keep it within the same boundaries as my understanding, but often stretch it to things I don't understand. Since my will remains neutral toward these things, it easily turns away from what is true and good, and as a result I am deceived and commit sin. For instance, when I recently examined whether anything exists, and discovered that from my very act of questioning this, it clearly follows that I myself exist, I couldn't help but judge what I so clearly understood to be true. This wasn't because any external force compelled me, but because a strong inclination in my will followed this great light in my understanding, so that I believed it all the more freely and willingly the less indifferent I felt about it. But now I understand not only that I exist as a thinking thing, but I also encounter a certain idea of physical nature, and it happens that I doubt whether the thinking nature within me differs from that physical nature, or whether they are one and the same. In this case, I suppose I have found no argument to lean me either way, and therefore I remain indifferent to affirm or deny either position, or to judge nothing about either. But this indifference extends not only to things about which I am clearly ignorant, but generally to all those things that aren't so very clearly known to me at the time when my will deliberates about them. For though highly probable assumptions may incline me toward one side, simply knowing that they are only conjectures and not indisputable reasons is enough to draw my assent toward the opposite side. I experienced this sufficiently recently when I regarded all those things I had previously accepted as most true to be very false, for this reason alone: that I found myself able to doubt them in some way.*

If I refrain from making a judgment when I do not perceive clearly and distinctly enough what is true, it is evident that I act correctly and am not deceived. But if I affirm or deny something, then I misuse the freedom of my will, and if I turn toward what is false, I am deceived. However, if I embrace the opposite position, it is only by chance that I arrive at the truth, yet I will not be blameless for this reason: it is clear by the natural light that the perception of the understanding should come before the determination of the will. And it is in this misuse of free will that the deprivation consists which constitutes error. I mean there is a deprivation in the action as it proceeds from me, but not in the faculty which I have received from God, nor in the action as it depends on him.

I don't have any reason to complain that God hasn't given me a greater intellectual capacity or more natural insight, because it's a necessary characteristic of a limited understanding that it cannot comprehend everything, and it's natural for a created understanding to be finite. I have more reason to thank him for what he has granted me (though he owed me nothing) than to think myself cheated by him of those things which he never gave me.

I have no reason to complain that God has given me a will that is larger than my understanding, because the will consists of only one thing and is essentially indivisible (namely, to will or not to will), so it seems contrary to its nature that it should be less than it is; and certainly, the greater it is, the more grateful I ought to be to the one who gave it to me.

I also cannot complain that God participates with me in producing those voluntary actions or judgments in which I am mistaken: for those acts, as they depend on God, are entirely true and good; and I am somewhat more perfect in being able to act this way than if I could not: for that absence, in which the formal essence of falsehood and sin consists, does not require God's participation; for it is not a thing, and when considered in relation to him as its cause, should not be called an absence, but rather a negation; for it is certainly no imperfection in God that he has given me the freedom to agree or disagree with certain things, the clear and distinct knowledge of which he has not granted to my understanding; but it is certainly an imperfection in me that I misuse this freedom and make judgments about things I do not properly understand.

Yet I see that it's possible for God to bring about that (though I should remain free, and possess finite knowledge) I should never make an error, that is, if he had given my understanding a clear and distinct knowledge of all things about which I should ever have occasion to deliberate; or if he had only so firmly established in my mind that I should never forget this: that I must never judge a thing which I do not clearly and distinctly understand. If God had done either of these things, I easily perceive that I (as considered in myself) would be more perfect than I now am, yet nevertheless I cannot deny that there may be a greater perfection in the whole universe of things, in that some of its parts are subject to errors, and some not, than if they were all alike. And I have no reason to complain that it has pleased God that I should play on the stage of this world a part not the chief and most perfect of all; or that I should not be able to avoid error in the first way specified above, which depends upon the evident knowledge of those things about which I deliberate. Yet I may avoid error by the other means mentioned above, which depends only on this: that I judge nothing whose truth is not evident. For though I have experienced in myself this weakness, that I cannot always focus upon one and the same knowledge, yet I may by continued and often repeated meditation bring this to pass, that as often as I have use of this rule I may remember it, by which means I may acquire (as it were) a habit of not erring.

Since I can see that the greatest and most important perfection of humanity lies in this understanding, I believe I have gained much from today's meditation, because through it I have discovered the cause of error and falsehood; this cause certainly can be nothing other than what I have just explained. Whenever I make a judgment and restrain my will so that it extends only to those things I clearly and distinctly perceive, it is impossible for me to make an error. Without doubt, every clear and distinct perception is something real, and therefore cannot come from nothing, but must necessarily have God as its author (God, I say, who is infinitely perfect and who cannot deceive), and therefore it must be true.

Today I have learned not only what I must guard against to avoid being deceived, but also what I must do to discover truth. I will certainly find truth if I focus entirely on those things I completely understand, and if I separate these from what I perceive only in a confused and unclear way. I will strive to do both of these things going forward.

MEDITATION V.

ON THE ESSENCE OF MATERIAL THINGS.
AND AGAIN ON GOD. AND THAT
HE DOES EXIST.

There are still many things remaining about God's attributes, and many things about the nature of myself or my mind, that should be investigated: but I will perhaps take these up at some other opportunity. And at present nothing seems more necessary to me (since I have discovered what I must avoid, and what I must do to attain truth) than to employ my efforts to free myself from those doubts into which I have recently fallen, and to try whether I can have any certainty about material things.

But before I investigate whether such things actually exist outside of me, I should examine the ideas of those things as they appear in my mind and determine which ones are clear and which ones are unclear.

In this search, I find that I clearly imagine Quantity, which Philosophers commonly call continuous, meaning the Extension of that Quantity or continuous thing into Length, Breadth, and Thickness. I can count various Parts within it, and to these parts I can assign Size, Shape, Position, and Local Motion, and to this Local Motion I can assign Duration. Not only are these general concepts clearly discovered and known by me, but also through careful consideration, I perceive countless particulars concerning the Shapes, Number, and Motion of these Bodies. The truth of these discoveries is so evident and natural to me that when I first discovered them, I didn't feel like I had learned something new, but rather that I had simply remembered what I already knew, or had merely reflected on things that were already within me, even though this was the first time I had examined them so carefully.

One thing deserves my consideration, which is that I find within myself countless ideas of certain things that, although they perhaps exist nowhere outside of me, cannot be said to be nothing; and although I think about them at my own will and pleasure, they are not created by me, but have their own true and unchanging natures. For instance, when I imagine a triangle, although such a figure perhaps exists nowhere outside my thoughts, nor ever will exist, its nature is still determined, and its essence or form is unchanging and eternal, which is neither created by me nor depends on my mind, as becomes clear from the fact that many properties can be demonstrated about this triangle—namely, that its three angles equal two right angles, that the greatest side lies opposite the greatest angle, and similar properties—which I now clearly understand whether I want to or not, even though I never thought about them before when I imagined a triangle, and consequently they could not have been invented by me. It serves no purpose for me to say that perhaps this idea of a triangle came to me through my sense organs because I have sometimes seen triangular-shaped objects; for I can think of countless other figures that I cannot suspect came through my senses, and yet I can demonstrate various properties of them, just as with a triangle, which are certainly all true, since I know them clearly, and therefore they are something, and not mere nothing, for it is evident that what is true is something.

I have now sufficiently demonstrated that what I clearly perceive is true. Even if I had not demonstrated this, the nature of my mind is such that I cannot help but give my consent to what I perceive so clearly, at least while I am perceiving it this way. I remember that in the past, when I relied most heavily on sensory objects, I held those truths to be most certain which I evidently perceived, such as those concerning shapes, numbers, and other parts of arithmetic and geometry, as well as whatever relates to pure and abstract mathematics.

Now therefore, if from this alone—that I can form the idea of something in my mind—it follows that whatever I clearly and distinctly perceive as belonging to a thing actually does belong to it, can I not draw from this an argument to prove the existence of God? I certainly find the idea of God, or an infinitely perfect being, as naturally within me as the idea of any geometric shape or number. I understand as clearly and distinctly that it belongs to God's nature always to exist, just as I know that whatever I can demonstrate about a mathematical figure or number belongs to the nature of that figure or number. Therefore, even if everything I have contemplated over these past three or four days were false, I could still be as certain of God's existence as I have been of mathematical truths.

Doubt. Yet this argument at first glance doesn't appear so obvious, but rather looks like a sophism; for since I am accustomed in all other things to distinguish existence from essence, I can easily convince myself that God's existence may be distinguished from his essence, so that I may imagine God not to exist.

Solution. But when we examine this more carefully, it becomes clear that God's existence cannot be separated from his essence any more than the equality of a triangle's three angles to two right angles can be separated from the essence of a triangle, or than the idea of a mountain can exist without the idea of a valley. Therefore, it is just as contradictory to think of a God (that is, a being infinitely perfect) who

*lacks existence (that is, who lacks a perfection) as it is to think of a
mountain that has no adjoining valley.*

*Doubt. But what if I cannot imagine God except as existing, or
a mountain without a valley? Yet supposing I think of a mountain
with a valley, it does not follow from this that there is a mountain in
the world; so supposing I think of God as existing, it still does not
follow that God really exists. For my thought imposes no necessity on
things, and just as I may imagine a winged horse, though no horse has
wings, so I may imagine an existing God, though no God exists.*

*Solution. It's true the fallacy seems to lie in this, yet though I
cannot conceive a mountain without a valley, it does not follow from
this that a mountain or valley actually exists, but this will follow, that
whether a mountain or valley exists or does not exist, they cannot be
separated: so from the fact that I cannot think of God except as existing,
it follows that existence is inseparable from God, and therefore that he
really exists; not because my thought accomplishes all this, or imposes
any necessity on anything, but on the contrary, because the necessity of
the thing itself (namely, of God's existence) determines me to think this
way; for it is not within my power to think of a God without existence
(that is, a being absolutely perfect without the chief perfection) as it is
within my power to imagine a horse either with or without wings.*

*Doubt. And here it cannot be said that I am forced to assume
God exists after I have assumed he possesses all perfections, since
existence is one of them; but rather that my first position (namely, his
absolute perfection) is not necessary. Thus, for example, it is not
necessary for me to think that all four-sided figures can be inscribed in
a circle; but supposing that I think so, I am then forced to admit that
a rhombus can be inscribed within it, and yet this is clearly false.*

*Solution. Although I am not compelled at any time to think of a
God, whenever I direct my thoughts toward a First and Supreme Being,
and essentially draw forth from the storehouse of my mind an idea of
such a being, I must necessarily attribute to it all kinds of perfections,
even though I do not at that moment enumerate them or notice each*

individual one. This necessity is sufficient to make me later (when I come to consider existence as a perfection) conclude correctly that the First and Supreme Being does exist. For instance, I am not required at any time to imagine a triangle, yet whenever I choose to consider a straight-sided figure having only three angles, I am then compelled to grant it all those properties from which I may rightly argue that its three angles are not greater than two right angles, even though this did not occur to me upon first consideration. But when I investigate what figures may be inscribed within a circle, I am not at all compelled to think that all four-sided figures are of that type; nor can I possibly imagine this, while I accept nothing except what I clearly and distinctly understand. Therefore there is a great difference between these false assumptions and true innate ideas, the first and supreme of which is that of a God. For in many ways I understand that this is not a fiction depending on my thought, but an image of a true and unchangeable nature. First, because I can think of no other thing except God to whose essence existence belongs. Second, because I cannot imagine two or more Gods, and assuming that only one exists now, I can clearly perceive it necessary for Him to have existed from eternity and to continue existing for eternity. And finally, because I perceive many other things in God which I cannot change and from which I cannot subtract.

But whatever method of reasoning I use, it all comes down to this one thing: I am completely convinced of the truth of only those things that appear to me clearly and distinctly. And although some of those things that I perceive this way are obvious to everyone, while others are discovered only by those who examine more closely and investigate more carefully, once such truths are discovered, they are considered no less certain than the others. For example, although it may not be as readily apparent that in a right-angled triangle, the square of the base equals the squares of the sides, as it is apparent that the base lies opposite the largest angle, the first proposition is believed no less certainly once it is understood than the second.

Thus in reference to God; certainly, unless I am overwhelmed with prejudice, or have my thoughts surrounded on all sides with physical objects, I should acknowledge nothing before or easier than him; For what is more self-evident than that there is a Supreme Being, or than that a God (to whose essence alone existence belongs) does exist? And though serious consideration is required to perceive this much, yet now, I am not only equally certain of it, as of what seems most certain, but I perceive also that the truth of other things so depends on it, that without it nothing can ever be perfectly known.

Although my nature is such that during the time of my clear and distinct perception, I cannot help but believe it to be true, my nature is also such that I cannot always fix my mind's attention on one and the same thing so as to perceive it clearly, and the memory of what judgment I have previously made is often brought up when I stop paying attention to those reasons for which I made such a judgment. Other reasons may then be presented which, if I did not know God, could easily change my opinion, and in this way I would never achieve true and certain knowledge of anything, but would have only wandering and unstable opinions. For example, when I consider the nature of a triangle, it clearly appears to me, as someone who understands the principles of geometry, that its three angles equal two right angles, and I must necessarily think this is true as long as I pay attention to its demonstration. But as soon as I withdraw my mind from considering its proof, even though I remember that I once clearly perceived it, I might still doubt its truth if I remain ignorant of God. I might convince myself that I am naturally designed to be deceived in those things which I imagine myself to perceive most clearly, especially when I recall that I have often previously considered many things to be true and certain which I later judged to be false based on other reasons. But when I perceive that there is a God, because at the same time I also understand that all things depend on him and that he is not a deceiver, and when I conclude from this that all those things which I clearly and distinctly perceive are necessarily true, then even though I no longer focus on those reasons which led me to believe it was true, if I simply remember that I once clearly and distinctly perceived it, no contrary argument can be brought forward that would make me doubt that I have true and certain knowledge of it. And not only of that, but of all other truths as well which I remember having once demonstrated, such as geometrical propositions and similar matters.

What objections can now be raised against me? Should I claim that nature has made me prone to frequent deception? No, because I now understand that I cannot be deceived about things I clearly comprehend. Should I argue that I have previously considered many things to be true and certain, only to later discover they were false? No, because I never perceived those things clearly and distinctly. Being unaware of this rule of truth, I accepted them based on reasoning that I later found to be weak. What else could be said? Should I claim, as I recently objected, that perhaps I am dreaming, and that my current thoughts are no more true than the dreams of sleeping people? But this possibility doesn't shake my conviction, because even if I were asleep, anything that appeared evident to my understanding would still be true.

And so I clearly see that the certainty and truth of all knowledge depends on knowing the true God, so that before I knew Him, I knew nothing at all; but now many things about God himself, and about other intellectual matters, as well as about physical nature, which is the subject of mathematics, can be clearly known and certain to me.

MEDITATION VI.

ON PHYSICAL THINGS AND THEIR EXISTENCE: AND ALSO ON THE REAL DISTINCTION BETWEEN MIND AND BODY.

Now I need to examine whether any physical beings actually exist. I already know that they can exist (at least in principle) since they are the subject of pure mathematics, and I perceive them clearly and distinctly. Without doubt, God has the power to create whatever I am able to perceive, and I have never considered anything to be beyond his power except what contradicted a clear perception. Furthermore, such material beings appear to exist based on the faculty of imagination, which I find myself using when I think about them. When I carefully consider what imagination is, it seems to be simply a particular application of our cognitive or knowing faculty to a body or object that stands before it. If it stands before it, then it must exist.

But to make this clearer, I must first examine the difference between imagination and pure intellection, or understanding. So, for example, when I imagine a triangle, I do not only understand that it is a figure enclosed by three lines, but I also see with my mind's eye those three lines as if they were before me, and this is what I call imagination. But if I turn my thoughts to a chiliagon, or figure consisting of a thousand angles, I know just as well that this is a figure enclosed by a thousand sides, as I know that a triangle is a figure consisting of three sides; but I do not in the same way imagine, or see as present those thousand sides, as I do the three sides of a triangle. And though at the time when I think of a chiliagon, I may confusedly represent to myself some figure (because whenever I think of a physical object, I am accustomed to imagine some shape or other) yet it is evident that this representation is not a chiliagon, because it is in no way different from what I would represent to myself if I thought of a million-angled figure, or any other figure with more sides; nor does such a confused representation help me in the least to know those properties by which a chiliagon differs from other polygons or many-angled figures. But if a question is asked concerning a pentagon, I know I can understand its shape, as I understand the shape of a chiliagon, without the help of imagination, but I can also imagine it, by directing my mind's eye to its five sides, and to the area or space contained by them; and in this I clearly perceive that there is required a particular kind of operation in the mind to imagine a thing, which I do not require to understand a thing; this new operation of the mind clearly shows the difference between imagination and pure intellection.

Besides this, I consider that this power of imagination within me (as it differs from the power of understanding) does not belong to the essence of me, that is, of my mind, for though I lacked it, I would certainly still be the same person that I am now: from this it seems to follow that it depends on something different from myself; and I easily perceive that if any body whatsoever did exist, to which my mind were so joined that it may apply itself when it pleased to consider, or (as it were) look into this body; from this, I say, I perceive it may be so, that by this very body I may imagine corporeal beings: So that this manner of thinking differs from pure intellection only in this, that the mind, when it understands, does as it were turn itself to itself, or reflect on itself, and beholds some or other of those ideas which are in itself; but when it imagines, it converts itself upon body, and therein beholds something conformable to that idea which it has understood, or perceived by sense.

But it should be remembered that I said I can easily understand how imagination might work, assuming that physical bodies exist. And since no more convenient way of explaining it presents itself, I probably conclude from this that physical bodies do exist. But I only say this is probable, because even though I should carefully examine all the arguments drawn from the distinct idea of physical body that I find in my imagination, I still find none of them from which I can necessarily conclude that physical bodies actually exist.

But I have grown accustomed to imagining many other things beyond that physical nature which serves as the subject of pure mathematics; things like colors, sounds, tastes, pain, and so forth, though none of these as clearly. And since I perceive these things better through the senses, from which they reach the imagination with the help of memory, so that I may deal with them more effectively, I should at the same time examine sensation itself, and determine whether from what I perceive through that mode of thinking which I call sensation, I can derive any reliable proof for the existence of physical objects.

And first, I will reflect on what those things were that I previously believed to be true based on what I perceived through my senses, and the reasons why I thought this way. I will then examine the reasons that later led me to doubt those things. And finally, I will consider what I should think about those things now.

First, I have always believed that I possess a head, hands, feet, and other body parts that make up this body, which I have considered either as part of myself or perhaps as my entire self. I have also believed that my body exists among many other bodies that can affect it in ways that are either beneficial or harmful. I determined what was beneficial through a feeling of pleasure, and what was harmful through a feeling of pain. Moreover, in addition to pleasure and pain, I experienced within myself hunger, thirst, and other similar appetites, as well as certain physical tendencies toward joy, sadness, anger, and other comparable emotions.

Regarding what happened to me from external bodies, besides the extension, shape, and movement of those bodies, I also perceived in them hardness, heat, and other qualities that could be felt through touch, as well as light, colors, smells, tastes, sounds, and so forth, and through the variation of these qualities I distinguished the heavens, earth, and seas, and all other bodies from one another.

It wasn't entirely unreasonable for me to think this way, given these ideas about qualities that presented themselves to my mind and that I directly and immediately perceived. I believed I was perceiving things that existed separately from my thoughts—namely, the physical bodies or objects that these ideas might come from. I often noticed that these ideas appeared in my mind without my permission or intention. I couldn't perceive an object, even when I wanted to, unless it was actually present before my sense organs. Similarly, I couldn't prevent myself from perceiving something when it was right there in front of me.

And since the ideas I receive through my senses are much more vivid, clear, and distinct in their own way than any of those I consciously and deliberately create through meditation or recall from my memory, it appears to me that they cannot originate from myself. Therefore, there remains no other way for them to reach me except from some other things outside of me. Since I have no other knowledge of these things except through these ideas, I cannot help but think that these ideas resemble the things themselves.

Moreover, I remember that I first used my senses before I developed my reasoning abilities; and because I noticed that the ideas I created myself were not as clear as those I received through my senses, but were very often composed of parts from sensory experience, I was easily convinced to believe that I had no idea in my mind that I had not first experienced through my senses.

Neither was it without reason that I judged that body (which by a special right I call my own) to be more closely connected to me than any other body. For I can never be separated from it, as I can from other bodies, I was aware of all appetites and feelings in it and for it, and finally I perceived pleasure and pain in its parts, and not in any other body outside it. But why a certain grief should arise in the mind from the sensation of pain, and a certain joy from the sensation of pleasure, or why that gnawing of the stomach, which I call hunger, should remind me of eating, or the dryness of my throat of drinking, I can give no other reason except that I am taught so by nature. For in my thinking there is no connection or similarity between that gnawing of the stomach and the desire of eating, or between the sensation of pain and the sorrowful thought that arises from it. But in this as in all other judgments that I made about sensible objects, I seemed to be taught by nature, for I first convinced myself that things were this way or that way, before I ever looked into a reason that might prove it.

But later I discovered many experiments where my senses deceived me so badly that I would never trust them again. Towers that appeared round from far away looked square when I got close, and large statues on top of them seemed small to people standing on the ground. In countless other situations, I realized that the judgments of my external senses were wrong—and not just my external senses, but my internal ones as well. What could be more intimate or internal than pain? Yet I have heard from people whose arms or legs were amputated that they still felt pain in the missing limb. Therefore, I cannot be completely certain that any part of me is actually experiencing pain, even though I feel pain there. To these doubts I have recently added two very general reasons for uncertainty. The first was that while I was awake, I could not believe I was perceiving anything that I might not also think I was perceiving while asleep. Since I cannot believe that what I seem to perceive in my dreams comes from external objects, what greater reason do I have to think this about what I perceive while awake? The second cause of doubt was that since I do not know who created me (or at least I assumed then that I did not know), what reason is there to think that I might not be designed by nature to be deceived even about those things that seemed most true to me? As for the reasons that led me to trust sensory experiences, it was easy to respond to them. Since I found through experience that nature drove me toward many things that reason advised against, I thought I should not place much trust in what nature taught me. And although my sensory perceptions did not depend on my will, I thought I should not conclude from this that they came from objects separate from myself. Perhaps there might be some other faculty within me, though still unknown to me, that could create those perceptions.

But now that I'm beginning to better understand myself and the Author of my origin, I don't think that everything I seem to receive from my senses should be rashly accepted, nor should everything be doubted. First, because I know that whatever I clearly and distinctly perceive can be created by God exactly as I perceive it; the ability to understand one thing clearly and distinctly without another is enough to make me certain that one thing is different from the other, because it can at least be separated by God, and for it to be considered different, it doesn't matter by what power it might be separated. Therefore, from my knowledge that I myself exist, and because at the same time I understand that nothing else belongs to my nature or essence except that I am a thinking being, I correctly conclude that my essence consists solely in this: that I am a thinking thing. And although perhaps (or, as I will show shortly, it's certain) I have a body that is very closely joined to me, yet because on one hand I have a clear and distinct idea of myself as only a thinking thing, not extended; and on the other hand because I have a distinct idea of my body as only an extended thing, not thinking, it is therefore certain that I am truly distinct from my body, and that I can exist without it.

Moreover, I find within myself certain faculties equipped with particular ways of thinking, such as the faculty of imagination and the faculty of perception or sensation. I can clearly and distinctly conceive of my entire self without these faculties, but I cannot conceive of these faculties without conceiving of myself—that is, an understanding substance in which they exist. None of these faculties in their formal conception includes understanding, which shows me that they are as different from me as the mode or manner of a thing is different from the thing itself.

I also recognize that I have several other abilities, such as changing location, taking on various forms, and so forth. These abilities cannot be understood without a substance in which they exist, any more than the previously mentioned abilities can, and therefore they cannot be understood to exist without that substance. However, it is clear that these types of abilities, in order for them to exist, must be present in a corporeal, extended substance, and not in an understanding substance, because extension, and not intellection or understanding, is included in the clear and distinct conception of them.

But I also possess a certain passive faculty of sensation, or of receiving and recognizing the ideas of sensible things. I could make no use of this faculty unless there existed within myself, or in something else, a certain active faculty capable of producing and creating those ideas. However, this active faculty cannot exist within myself, since it presupposes no understanding, and these ideas are produced in me without my assistance, and often against my will. Therefore, no place remains for this active faculty except that it should exist in some substance different from me. Since all the reality that is contained objectively in the ideas produced by that faculty ought to be contained formally or eminently (as I have previously observed), this substance must be either a body (in which what exists in the ideas objectively is contained formally) or it must be God, or some creature more excellent than a body (in which what exists in the ideas objectively is contained eminently). But since God is not a deceiver, it is altogether clear that he does not place these ideas in me either immediately from himself, or through the mediation of any other creature in which their objective reality is not contained formally, but only eminently. And since God has given me no faculty to discern whether these ideas proceed from corporeal or incorporeal beings, but rather a strong inclination to believe that they are sent from corporeal beings, there would be no reason why God should not be considered a deceiver if these ideas came from anywhere other than from corporeal things. Therefore we must conclude that there are corporeal beings. These may perhaps not all be exactly the same as I comprehend them through my senses (for perception through the senses is in many things very obscure and confused), but those things at least which I clearly and distinctly understand, that is to say, all those things which are comprehended under the object of pure mathematics—those things I say at least are true.

As for what remains, these are either specific details, such as the sun being of a particular size or shape, and so on, or they are things less clearly understood, such as light, sound, pain, and so forth. And though these and similar things may be very doubtful and uncertain, yet because God is not a deceiver, and because therefore none of my opinions can be false unless God has given me some faculty or other to correct my error, it is for this reason that I am encouraged with the hope of attaining truth even in these very things.

And it certainly cannot be questioned that whatever Nature teaches me contains some element of truth. When I speak of Nature in general, I mean either God himself, or the ordered arrangement of creatures created by God. When I refer to my own nature in particular, I mean the combination or collection of all those things that God has given to me.

Now there is nothing that my nature teaches me more clearly than that I have a body, which is not well when I feel pain, that this body needs food or drink when I am hungry or thirsty, and so on. Therefore I should not doubt that these things are true. Through this sense of pain, hunger, thirst, and so forth, my nature tells me that I am not in my body as a sailor is in his ship, but that I am most closely joined to it, and as it were blended with it; so that I and it make up one thing. Otherwise, when the body were injured, I, who am only a thinking thing, would not therefore feel pain, but would only perceive the injury with the eye of my understanding (as a sailor perceives by his sight whatever is broken in his ship) and when the body needs either food or drink, I would only understand this need, but would not have the confused sense of hunger or thirst. I call them confused, for certainly the sense of thirst, hunger, pain, and so on are only confused modes or ways of thought arising from the union and (as it were) mixture of the mind and body.

I am also taught by nature that there are many other bodies outside and around my body, some of which should be desired, while others should be avoided. Because I perceive very different colors, sounds, smells, tastes, heat, hardness, and similar qualities, I rightly conclude that there are corresponding differences in the bodies from which these different sense perceptions arise, though perhaps not exactly alike. Since some of these perceptions are pleasant while others are unpleasant, it is clearly certain that my body, or rather my whole self (as I am composed of mind and body), is capable of being affected by these bodies that surround me.

There are many other things that nature also seems to teach me, but I'm not really taught by it—instead, I've acquired them through the poor habit of making judgments carelessly, which is why these things often turn out to be false. For example, I assume that all space where I find nothing affecting my senses is empty; that in a hot object there exists something similar to the idea of heat that I experience; that in a white or green object there exists the same whiteness or greenness that I perceive; and that a bitter or sweet thing contains the same taste I experience, and so on. I also assume that stars, castles, and other distant objects are the same size and shape as they appear to my senses, along with similar assumptions. But to avoid accepting anything in this matter that I cannot clearly perceive, I need to determine more precisely what I mean when I say that nature teaches me something.

Here I understand Nature more specifically, as the combination of all those things that God has given me. Within this combination, there are many elements that relate to the mind alone, such as my perception that what has been done cannot be undone, and all other things that are known through natural understanding, but I am not discussing these at the moment. There are also many other things that belong only to the body, such as its tendency to fall downward and similar properties, but I am not addressing these right now either. Instead, I speak only of those things that God has given me as I am composed of both mind and body together, not considered separately. It is Nature, understood in this way, that teaches me to avoid troubling experiences and seek out pleasant ones. However, it does not appear that this Nature teaches us to draw any conclusions from these sensory perceptions before we conduct a careful examination of external objects through our reasoning. The task of investigating the truth of things does not belong to the complete human being as a combination of mind and body, but to the mind alone.

So even though a star affects my eye no more than a small spark of fire, there is in my eye no real or positive inclination to believe one is no bigger than the other, but I have been accustomed to judge this way from my childhood without any reason: and though coming near the fire I feel heat, and coming too near I feel pain, yet there is no reason to persuade me that in the fire there is anything like either that heat or that pain, but only that there is something within it, whatever it may be, that excites in us those sensations of heat or pain: and so though in some space there may be nothing that works on my senses, it does not follow from this that there is no body there; for I see that in these and many other things I am accustomed to overturn the order of nature, because I use these perceptions of sense (which properly are given me by nature to make known to the mind what is advantageous or harmful to the composite, of which the mind is part, and so far only they are clear and distinct enough) as certain rules immediately to discover the essence of external bodies, of which they make known nothing but very obscurely and confusedly.

I have previously shown how my judgment can be false despite God's goodness. But now a new difficulty arises concerning those very things which nature tells me I should pursue or avoid, concerning my internal senses, in which I find many errors, as when a man being deceived by the pleasant taste of some kind of food, consumes hidden poison within it. But in this very instance it cannot be said that the man is driven by nature to desire the poison, for he is completely unaware of that; but he is said to desire the food only because it has a pleasing taste; and from this nothing can be concluded except that human nature is not all-knowing; which is no wonder since man is a finite being, and therefore only finite perfections belong to him.

But we often make mistakes even in those things that nature drives us to do, like when sick people crave food or drink that will definitely harm them. Someone might respond that they make these mistakes because their nature is corrupted. But this doesn't solve the problem, because a sick person is just as much God's creation as a healthy person, and therefore it's equally absurd to imagine that

God would impose a deceptive nature on one rather than the other. Just as a clock made of wheels and weights follows the laws of its nature just as strictly when it's poorly designed and tells time incorrectly as when it fulfills the craftsman's intentions in every way, so too if I think of a human body as simply a machine or mechanism made up of bones, nerves, muscles, veins, blood, and skin—so that even if there were no mind in it, it would still perform all the same movements it does now (except for those that come from the will, and therefore from the mind)—I can easily recognize that it would be just as natural for this person (if, for example, he had dropsy) to experience the dryness in his throat that usually creates the sensation of thirst in his mind, and for his nerves and other parts to be arranged in such a way that he would drink, which would make his disease worse, as it would be natural (assuming he had no such illness) for similar throat dryness to make him want to drink when it's actually necessary. And although, if I consider the intended purpose of a clock, I might say it deviates from its nature when it tells time incorrectly, and similarly, thinking of a human body's movement as designed for the motions it usually performs, I might think it also deviates from its nature if its throat is dry when it doesn't actually need drink for its survival. Yet I clearly see that this second understanding of nature is very different from the one we've been discussing all along, because this one is only a label applied from outside to the things we're talking about, depending on my thoughts as I compare a sick person and a broken clock with the idea of a healthy person and a properly working clock. But by nature in its earlier meaning, I understand something that actually exists in the things themselves, which therefore contains some truth.

Although it may only be an external label to say that the nature of a body suffering from dropsy is corrupt because it has a dry throat and doesn't need drink, when we consider the complete combination of mind joined to such a body, it's not merely a label but a genuine error of nature for it to feel thirst when drinking would be harmful. Therefore, the question that remains to be examined here is how God's goodness allows nature, understood in this way, to be deceived.

First, I understand that a fundamental difference between my mind and body lies in this: my body is by its nature divisible, while my mind is indivisible. When I consider my mind or myself as merely a thinking being, I cannot distinguish any parts within me, but I perceive myself to be one complete entity. Although the entire mind appears to be united with the entire body, when a foot, an arm, or any other part of the body is severed, I do not conceive that any part of my mind has been removed. Similarly, the faculties of desiring, perceiving, understanding, and so forth cannot be called parts of the mind, because it is one and the same mind that desires, perceives, and understands. In contrast, I cannot think of any physical or extended being that I cannot easily divide into parts through my thought, and through this I understand it to be divisible. This fact alone, even if I had learned it from no other argument, would be sufficient to inform me that my mind is truly distinct from my body.

Next, I discover that my mind is not directly influenced by every part of my body, but only by the brain, and perhaps only by one small section of it—specifically, the area where common sense is said to be located. Whenever this part is arranged in the same way, it will present the same thing to the mind, even though the other parts of the body may be organized differently at that moment. This is demonstrated by countless experiments, which do not need to be described here.

Moreover, I discover that my body's nature is such that no part of it can be moved by another distant part without also being moved in the same way by some of the parts in between, even though the more distant part remains still and doesn't act; for example, in a rope,

$$A—B—C—D$$

if its end D. were pulled, the end A. would move in exactly the same way as if one of the middle parts B. or C. were pulled, while the end D. remained still. So when I feel pain in my foot, my understanding of physics teaches me that this happens through the help of nerves spread throughout the foot, which continue like ropes all the way to the brain, and when they are pulled in the foot, they also pull the inner parts of the brain that they connect to, creating a specific motion there that nature has designed to make the mind feel a sensation of pain, as if it were in the foot. But since these nerves must travel through the shin, the thighs, the lower back, the spine, and the neck before they can reach the brain from the foot, it's possible that even though the part of them in the foot isn't touched, but only some of their middle sections are affected, the same motion would still occur in the brain as when the foot itself is injured, which would necessarily result in the mind experiencing the same pain. And we can think about any other sense in the same way.

I finally understand that since each individual motion performed in that part of the brain which directly affects the mind produces only one type of sensation, nothing could be designed more efficiently than having it generate the sensation that primarily and most frequently contributes to maintaining a healthy person out of all the possible sensations it could create. Experience confirms that nature has given us all our senses for precisely this purpose, and therefore nothing can be discovered in them that does not clearly demonstrate God's power and goodness. For instance, when the nerves in our feet are violently and unusually stimulated, that motion travels through the spinal cord to the inner regions of the brain, where it signals to the mind that something should be felt—and what is this sensation but pain, as though it originates in the foot, which motivates the mind to work toward removing the cause since it threatens the foot's wellbeing. However, God could have designed human nature so that this same brain motion would present any other sensation to the mind—either the motion itself as it exists in the brain, or as it exists in the foot, or in any of the other intermediate parts mentioned earlier, or finally any other sensation imaginable. Yet none of these alternatives would have contributed as effectively to preserving the body. Similarly, when we need to drink, a certain dryness develops in the throat that stimulates its nerves, and through them the inner parts of the brain, and this motion creates the sensation of thirst in the mind, because in this situation nothing is more essential for us to recognize than our need for drink to maintain our health. The same principle applies to everything else.

From all of this, it's clear that despite God's infinite goodness, human nature—consisting of both mind and body—must inevitably be subject to deception. If any cause were to stimulate not the foot itself, but the brain directly, or any other part along the pathway where nerves extend from the foot to the brain, producing the same motion that typically arises when the foot is injured, pain would be felt as if it were in the foot, and our senses would naturally be deceived. This makes sense because that same brain motion always presents the same sensation to the mind, and since it more often results from something harmful to the foot than from any other cause, it's reasonable that it should signal foot pain to the mind rather than pain in any other part. Similarly, if throat dryness occurs not from the usual need for drink to maintain the body's health, but from an abnormal cause, as happens in dropsy, it's much better that our senses deceive us in that instance than that they should constantly deceive us when the body is healthy, and the same principle applies to everything else.

This understanding helps me greatly, not only to comprehend the mistakes my nature tends to make, but also to correct and prevent them. Since I know that my senses more often mislead me than tell me the truth about things that benefit my body, and since I can usually use more than one sense to examine the same thing, along with my memory that connects present and past experiences, and my understanding that has already revealed all the causes of my errors, I should no longer fear that what my senses show me daily might be false. Most importantly, those extreme doubts from my First Meditation should be dismissed as absurd, particularly the main one about not being able to distinguish sleep from waking. Now I clearly see a great difference between them, because my dreams are never connected by my memory with the other actions of my life the way everything that happens to me while awake is. Certainly, if while I were awake someone suddenly appeared to me and immediately vanished as happens in dreams, so that I couldn't tell where they came from or where they went, I would consider it a ghost or vision created by my brain rather than a real person. But when things happen that I clearly understand—knowing where, when, and how they occur—and I connect my perception of them through memory with the other events of my life, I am certain they are presented to me while awake and not asleep. I shouldn't doubt their truth in the slightest, especially if after calling upon all my senses, memory, and understanding to examine them, I find nothing that conflicts with other truths. Since God is not a deceiver, it follows that in such matters I am not being deceived. However, because the pressing demands of action in everyday affairs don't always allow time for such careful examination, I must admit that human life is prone to many errors regarding specific details, and we must acknowledge the weakness of our nature.

ADVERTISEMENT

CONCERNING THE OBJECTIONS.

Among seven sets of objections made by various learned individuals against these Meditations, I have chosen the third from the Latin edition, as it was written by Thomas Hobbes of Malmesbury, a man widely known throughout the world, but particularly to his own English nation; therefore it is likely that what comes from him may be more acceptable to his countrymen than what comes from a foreigner; and just as the strength of a fortress is never better understood than through forceful resistance, so it is with these Meditations which remain unshaken by the violent opposition of such a powerful adversary. Yet it must be acknowledged that the force of these objections and the compelling nature of the arguments cannot be properly understood by those who are not familiar with other works of Mr. Hobbes's philosophy, especially his books De Corpore and De Homine, the former of which I am certain has been translated into English, and therefore is not inappropriately referenced here in a discussion for English readers. This is the reason that makes the great Descartes pass over many of these objections so lightly, who certainly would have undermined the entire structure of Hobbesian philosophy had he only known upon what foundations it was built.

OBJECTIONS
Made against the Foregoing
MEDITATIONS,

BY THE FAMOUS
THOMAS HOBBES
Of Malmesbury,

WITH
DESCARTES'S
ANSWERS.

OBJECTION I.

AGAINST THE FIRST MEDITATION: CONCERNING THINGS THAT CAN BE CALLED INTO DOUBT.

It's clear enough from what has been discussed in this Meditation that there is no sign by which we can distinguish our dreams from true sensation and waking experience, and therefore those images that we have while awake and from our senses are not qualities inherent in external objects, nor do they prove that such external objects actually exist; and therefore if we rely on our senses without any other foundation, we may reasonably doubt whether anything exists or not. We therefore acknowledge the truth of this Meditation. But because Plato and other ancient philosophers argued for the same uncertainty regarding sensible things, and because it is commonly observed by ordinary people that it is difficult to distinguish sleep from waking, I would not want the most excellent author of such innovative ideas to present such ancient concepts.

Response

Those reasons for doubt that this philosopher accepts as true were presented by me only as probable possibilities, and I used them not to promote them as original ideas, but partly to prepare my readers' minds for contemplating intellectual matters, where these doubts seemed to me quite essential. I also used them partly to demonstrate how solid those truths are that I will establish later, since they cannot be undermined by these metaphysical doubts. Therefore, I never intended to gain any recognition by restating them, but I believe I could no more leave them out than a medical writer can skip describing a disease whose treatment he plans to explain.

OBJECTION II.

AGAINST THE SECOND MEDITATION: ON THE NATURE OF THE HUMAN MIND.

I am a thinking being. This is true; because I think or have an imagination (whether I am awake or asleep), it follows that I am thinking, since "I think" and "I am thinking" mean the same thing. Because I think, it follows that I exist, for whatever thinks cannot be nothing. But when he adds that this means I am a mind, a soul, an understanding, or reason, I question his argument; it does not seem like a valid conclusion to say, "I am a thinking being, therefore I am thought itself," nor "I am an understanding being, therefore I am understanding itself." Using the same logic, I could conclude, "I am a walking being, therefore I am walking itself."

Therefore Descartes concludes that a thinking being and thought (which is the action of a thinking being) are identical; or at least that a thinking being and the intellect (which is the capacity of a thinking being) are the same thing. However, all philosophers make a distinction between the subject and its faculties and actions—that is, between its properties and its essence—because the thing itself is one matter, and its essence is another. It may therefore be that a thinking being is the subject that possesses a mind, reason, or understanding, and consequently it may be a physical thing, though the opposite is assumed here without proof.

Yet this reasoning forms the foundation of the conclusion that Descartes seeks to establish.

In the same Meditation, I know that I am, I ask, What am I whom I thus know? Certainly the knowledge of myself precisely so taken does not depend on those things whose existence I am yet ignorant of.

It's certain that knowing the proposition "I am" depends on "I think," as he has correctly informed us; but where do we get our knowledge of the proposition "I think"? Certainly only from this: that we cannot conceive any action without its subject, such as dancing without a dancer, knowledge without a knower, or thought without a thinker.

And from this it appears to follow that a thinking being is a physical being; for the subjects of all actions are understood only in a physical way, or in the manner of matter, as he himself demonstrates later through the example of a piece of wax, which while changing its color, consistency, shape, and other properties is still known to remain the same thing, that is, the same matter subject to so many changes. But I cannot conclude from another thought that I now think; for though a person may think that he has thought (which consists only in memory) yet it is altogether impossible for him to think that he now thinks, or to know, that he knows, for the question may be put infinitely, how do you know that you know, that you know, that you know? and so on.

Since the knowledge of the proposition "I am" depends on the knowledge of "I think," and this knowledge comes only from the fact that we cannot separate thought from thinking matter, it seems more likely that a thinking thing is material rather than immaterial.

Response

When I said, "That is a Mind, a Soul, an Understanding, Reason," and so on, I did not mean by these names just the faculties themselves, but rather the things that possess those faculties. This is always how the first two terms (mind and soul) are understood, and very often how the last two terms (understanding and reason) are understood as well. I have explained this so frequently and in so many places throughout these Meditations that there should be no reason to question what I mean.

Neither is there any similarity between walking and thought, because walking refers only to the action itself, but thought is sometimes used to describe the action, sometimes the ability, and sometimes the thing itself where that ability exists.

I'm not claiming that the thinking entity and the act of thinking are identical, nor that the thinking entity and the intellect are the same when intellect refers to a faculty. However, they are the same when intellect refers to the actual thing that thinks. I freely admit that I have deliberately used abstract terms to describe the thing or substance that I want to strip of all properties that don't essentially belong to it. In contrast, this philosopher employs the most concrete words to describe this thinking entity—terms like subject, matter, body, and so forth—to prevent it from being separated from the physical body.

I'm not concerned that his method of combining many things together might appear to some people more suitable for discovering truth than my approach, where I separate each particular element as much as possible. But let's set aside words and focus on the actual matters at hand.

He says that a thinking thing might be a physical thing, and claims that I assumed the opposite without proving it. But he's wrong about this, because I never assumed the contrary, nor did I use it as a foundation for the rest of my argument. Instead, I left it completely undetermined until the sixth Meditation, where it is actually proved.

Then he correctly tells us that we cannot imagine any action without its subject, such as thought without a thinking being, because what thinks cannot be nothing; however, he then adds without any justification, and against the normal way of speaking, and contrary to all logic, that from this it appears to follow that a thinking being is a physical entity. Indeed, the subjects of all actions are understood under the concept of substance, or if you prefer under the concept of matter (that is to say, metaphysical matter) but not therefore under the concept of bodies.

But logicians and generally all people are accustomed to saying that there are some spiritual and some corporeal substances. And through the example of wax I only demonstrated that color, consistency, shape, and so forth do not belong to the formal essence of the wax; for in that discussion I addressed neither the formal essence of the mind nor of the body.

Neither is it relevant to the matter that the Philosopher claims that one thought cannot be the subject of another thought, for who besides himself ever imagined this? But so I may explain the matter in a few words, it is certain that thought cannot exist without a thinking thing, nor can any act or any accident exist without a substance in which it resides. But since we do not know a substance directly by itself, but only by this alone, that it is the subject of several acts, it is very much in accordance with the commands of reason and custom that we should call by different names those substances which we perceive are the subjects of very different acts or accidents, and that afterwards we should examine whether those different names signify different things or one and the same thing. Now there are some acts which we call corporeal, such as magnitude, figure, motion, and whatever else cannot be thought of without local extension, and the substance in which these reside we call body; nor can it be imagined that it is one substance which is the subject of figure, and another substance which is the subject of local motion, and so on, because all these acts agree under one common notion of extension. Besides there are other acts, which we call cogitative or thinking, such as understanding, will, imagination, sense, and so on, all of which agree under the common notion of thought, perception, or consciousness; and the substance in which they exist, we say, is a thinking thing, or mind, or call it by whatever other name we please, so long as we do not confuse it with corporeal substance, because cogitative acts have no affinity with corporeal acts, and thought, which is the common principle of those, is wholly different from extension, which is the common principle of these. But after we have formed two distinct conceptions of these two substances, from what is said in the sixth meditation, it is easy to know whether they are one and the same or different.

OBJECTION III.

WHICH ONE OF THESE IS SEPARATE FROM MY THINKING? WHICH ONE CAN EXIST APART FROM ME?

Some people might answer this question by saying: I myself am the one who thinks, and I am distinct from my thoughts. My thoughts are different from me (though not separated from me), just as dancing is distinguished from the dancer (as noted earlier). But if Descartes wants to prove that the person who understands is the same as his understanding, we will fall back into the scholastic way of speaking, where the understanding understands, the sight sees, the will wills, and then by exact analogy, the walking (or at least the faculty of walking) shall walk. All of these expressions are unclear, inappropriate, and unworthy of the clarity that is typical of the noble Descartes.

Response

I don't deny that I, as the one who thinks, am distinct from my thoughts, just as a thing is distinguished from its mode or manner of being. But when I ask which of these is distinct from my thought, I'm referring to those various modes of thinking I mentioned, not to substance itself. And when I add the question of which of these can be separated from me, I'm simply indicating that all these modes or ways of thinking exist within me. I don't see what reason there could be for doubt or confusion about this point.

OBJECTION IV.

It remains therefore for me to confess that I cannot imagine what this wax is, but that I understand in my mind what it is.

There is a significant difference between imagination (that is, having an idea of something) and mental conception (that is, concluding through reasoning that something is or exists). However, Descartes has not explained to us how they differ. Furthermore, the ancient Aristotelians have clearly taught as doctrine that substance is not perceived through the senses but is gathered through logical reasoning.

But what should we say now if reasoning turns out to be nothing more than a linking or chaining together of names or terms through the word "is"? This would mean that when we gather conclusions through reasoning, we're not actually learning anything about the nature of things themselves, but only about the names we give to things. In other words, we're simply finding out whether we're connecting the names of things according to the agreements we've arbitrarily made about what they mean. If this is the case (and it very well might be), then reasoning depends on words, words depend on imagination, and imagination—along with our senses—might depend on the movement of physical parts of our bodies. This would mean that the mind is nothing more than movements happening in certain parts of a living, organized body.

Response

I have explained here the difference between imagination and pure mental conception by listing in my example of the wax what we imagine about it and what we conceive in our mind alone: but beyond this, I have explained elsewhere how we understand in one way, and imagine in another way, one and the same thing, such as a pentagon or five-sided figure.

There is in reasoning a connection not of words, but of the things that words represent; and I find it remarkable that anyone could think otherwise. Who has ever doubted that a French person and a German person can argue about the same subjects, even though they use very different words? And doesn't the philosopher contradict himself when he speaks of the agreements we have arbitrarily made about what words mean? If he acknowledges that words signify something, why won't he admit that our reasoning concerns this something rather than just words alone? By the same logic that leads him to conclude the mind is motion, he could just as easily conclude that the earth is heaven, or whatever else he chooses.

OBJECTION V.

AGAINST THE THIRD MEDITATION OF GOD.

Some of these human thoughts are like images of things, and only these properly deserve the name "idea" - such as when I think of a man, a chimera, heaven, an angel, or God.

When I think about a person, I perceive an idea composed of shape and color, and I may question whether this represents the likeness of an actual person or not; the same happens when I think about Heaven. However, when I think about a chimera, I perceive an image or idea that makes me wonder whether it resembles any animal that not only exists now, but could possibly exist, or that ever will exist in the future or not.

But when thinking about an Angel, my mind sometimes presents the image of a flame, and sometimes the image of a pretty little boy with wings. I am certain this bears no resemblance to an Angel, and therefore it is not the true idea of an Angel. However, believing that there are some creatures who serve God and are invisible and immaterial, we give the name Angel to this thing we believe or suppose to exist. Meanwhile, the idea under which I imagine an Angel is made up of ideas from things we can perceive with our senses.

In the same way, when we speak the sacred name of God, we have no image or idea of what God looks like, and therefore we are forbidden to worship God through any image, so that we don't appear to think we can understand Him who cannot be understood.

This shows that we have no real understanding of God; we're like someone born blind who is brought near a fire and feels the warmth, knowing that something is warming them. When they hear it called fire, they conclude that fire exists, but they don't know what shape or color the fire has, nor do they have any picture or concept of it in their mind.

So when people realize that there must be some cause behind their thoughts and ideas, and another cause before that one, and so on, they eventually reach an endpoint or assume there must be some eternal cause. Since this eternal cause never began to exist, it cannot have any other cause before it, and from this reasoning they conclude that some eternal thing must necessarily exist. Yet they have no clear concept that they can call the idea of this eternal thing, but they give this thing, which they believe in and acknowledge, the name God.

But now Descartes proceeds from this position, that we have an idea of God in our mind, to prove this theorem, that God (that is an almighty, wise, creator of the world) exists, whereas he ought to have explained this idea of God better, and he should have then deduced not only his existence, but also the creation of the world.

Response

Here the philosopher wants the word "idea" to be understood only as images of material things represented in a bodily imagination. With this position, he can easily prove that there can be no proper idea of an angel or God. However, as I declare everywhere, but especially in this place, I use the name "idea" for whatever is immediately perceived by the mind. So when I will something or fear something, because at the same time I perceive that I will or fear, this very act of willing or fearing is counted by me among the number of ideas. I have deliberately used that word because it was customary among the ancient philosophers to signify the manner of perceptions in the divine mind, although neither we nor they acknowledge an imagination in God. Besides, I had no better word to express it.

I believe I have adequately explained the concept of God for those who will pay attention to my meaning, but I can never do it thoroughly enough for those who will interpret my words differently than I intend them.

Finally, what is added here about the Creation of the World is completely irrelevant to the question at hand.

OBJECTION. VI.

But there are other thoughts that have additional forms attached to them, such as when I will something, when I fear, when I affirm, or when I deny. I know that whenever I think, I always have some particular thing as the subject or object of my thought, but in this latter type of thoughts there is something more that I think about than simply the resemblance of the thing. Some of these thoughts are called wills and emotions, while others are called judgments.

When anyone experiences fear or desire, they certainly have a mental image of the thing they fear or the action they want, but what else goes through the mind of someone who is afraid or wanting something isn't clearly explained. Although fear is a thought, I don't see how it can be anything other than the thought of the thing being feared.

What is the fear of a lion charging at me, except the idea of a lion charging at me, and the effect that this idea creates in the heart, which drives the fearful person to that instinctive movement we call running away? But this act of fleeing isn't a thought itself, so it follows that in fear there is no other thought except the one that resembles the actual thing. The same principle applies to desire.

Furthermore, affirmation and negation require voice and words, which is why animals cannot affirm or deny anything, not even in their thoughts, and therefore they cannot make judgments. However, the same thought can exist in an animal as in a human being; when we affirm that a person is running, our thought is not different from what a dog experiences when it sees its master running. Affirmation or negation, therefore, adds nothing to pure thoughts, except perhaps it adds the thought that the names making up an affirmation are (to the person making the affirmation) names for the same thing; this does not mean understanding more about the thing in thought than its likeness, but rather understanding the same likeness twice.

Response

It's obvious that seeing a lion while simultaneously fearing it is one thing, and simply seeing the lion is another thing entirely. Similarly, it's one thing to see a man running, and quite another thing to affirm to myself (which can be done silently) that I see him.

But in all this objection I find nothing that requires an answer.

OBJECTION VII.

*Now it remains for me to examine how I have received this idea of God, for I have neither received it through my senses, nor does it come to me without my deliberate thought, as the ideas of sensible things usually do when those things act upon the organs of my senses, or at least appear to act upon them. This idea is not created by myself either, for I can neither add to it nor take away from it. Therefore, I can only conclude that it is innate, just as the idea of myself is natural to me.

If there is no idea of God, as it appears there is not (and here it is not proven that there is), this entire discussion collapses. And regarding the idea of myself (if I consider the body), it comes from sight, but (if the soul) there is no idea of a soul, but we conclude through reasoning that there is some inner thing in a person's body that gives it living motion, by which it perceives and moves, and this (whatever it may be) without any idea we call a soul.

Response

If there is an Idea of God (as it is clear that there is) this entire objection collapses; and then he adds that we have no Idea of the Soul, but gather it through reasoning. This is the same as if he were to say that there is no image of it represented in the imagination, but yet that there is such a thing as what I call an Idea.

OBJECTION VIII.

Another idea about the Sun, drawn from the arguments of astronomers, which I have logically gathered from certain natural concepts.

At the same time, we can certainly have only one idea of the Sun, whether we look at it with our eyes or determine through reasoning that it is much bigger than it appears; for this reasoning is not an idea of the Sun, but proof through arguments that the idea of the Sun would be much larger if we looked at it from closer. But at different or separate times, the ideas of the Sun may be diverse, as if at one time we look at it with our naked eye, at another time through a telescope; but astronomical arguments do not make the idea of the Sun greater or smaller, but they rather tell us that the sensible idea of it is false.

Response

Here also (just as before) what he describes is not the Idea of the Sun, and yet what is described is that very thing which I call the Idea.

OBJECTION IX.

*For without doubt, those ideas that represent substances contain something more, or (as I may say) possess more objective reality in them, than those that represent only accidents or modes; and again, that by which I understand a supreme God, Eternal, Infinite, All-knowing, All-powerful, Creator of all things besides himself, certainly has in it more objective reality than those by which finite substances are displayed.

I have previously noted on several occasions that there can be no idea of God or the mind. I will now add that there can be no idea of substance either. Substance, which is simply matter subject to accidents and changes, can only be understood through reasoning, but it cannot be conceived at all, nor does it present any idea to us. If this is true, how can it be claimed that those ideas which represent substances to us contain something more, or possess greater objective reality, than those ideas which represent accidents to us? Furthermore, let Descartes reconsider what he means by "more reality." Can reality be increased or decreased? Or does he believe that one thing can be more of a thing than another thing? Let him consider how this can be explained to our understanding with the clarity and precision that is required in all demonstrations, and which he himself typically provides on other occasions.

Response

I have often noted before that the very thing which is evidenced by reason, as well as whatever else is perceived by any other means, is called by me an idea. And I have sufficiently explained how reality may be increased or diminished, in the same manner (that is to say) as substance is more a thing than a mode; and if there are any such things as real qualities, or incomplete substances, these are more things than modes, and less things than complete substances: and lastly if there is an infinite independent substance this is more a thing than a finite, dependent substance. And all this is self-evident.

OBJECTION. X.

Therefore, only the idea of God remains; here I must

consider whether there is something included that could not possibly have originated from me. By the word God, I mean a certain infinite substance, independent, all-knowing, all-powerful, by whom both I myself and everything else that exists (if anything actually exists) was created. All these attributes are of such a lofty nature that the more carefully I examine them, the less I can conceive that I alone could possibly be the author of these concepts; from what has therefore been said, I must conclude that there is a God.

Considering the attributes of God, so that we may form an understanding of God and investigate whether there might be something in that understanding which could not possibly come from ourselves, I find (if I am not mistaken) that what we conceive when we hear the revered name of God comes neither from ourselves, nor is it necessary that these concepts should have any other source than external objects. When I use the name of God, I mean a substance—that is, I understand that God exists (not through an idea, but through reasoning)—infinite (meaning I cannot conceive or imagine boundaries or parts in him so extreme that I cannot imagine others beyond them), from which it follows that what presents itself at the word infinite is not an idea of God's infinity but rather an awareness of my own boundaries and limitations. Independent—that is, I do not conceive of any cause from which God might originate; from this it is clear that I have no other idea when I hear the word independent except the memory of my own ideas, which at different times have different beginnings, and therefore they must be dependent.

Therefore, to say that God is independent is simply to say that God is among those things whose origin I cannot imagine: and similarly, to say that God is infinite is the same as saying that He is among those things whose limits we cannot conceive: And in this way any idea of God is destroyed, for what idea can we have of something without beginning or end?

Omniscient or Understanding all things. Here I want to know what idea Descartes uses to understand God's Understanding? Almighty. I also want to know what idea is used to understand God's Power? Power relates to future things—that is, things that don't exist yet. For my part, I understand power through the image or memory of past actions, reasoning with myself like this: He did that, so he was able (or had the power) to do it, therefore (following the same logic) he will have the power to do it again. But all of these are ideas that can come from external objects.

Creator of all things, I can form an image of Creation from what I observe every day, like a man being born, or growing from a tiny point to the shape and size he now possesses; no person can have any other idea than this when hearing the word Creator; But the ability to imagine a Creation is not enough to prove that the world was created. And therefore even if it were proven that some Infinite Independent Almighty Being did exist, it would not follow from this that a Creator exists; unless someone can consider this to be a valid inference, we believe that there exists something that has created all other things, therefore the world was Created by it.

Furthermore, when he claims that the idea of God and of our soul is innate or born within us, I would like to know whether the souls of those who sleep deeply actually think unless they are dreaming. If they do not think during deep sleep, then at that moment they possess no ideas, and therefore no idea can be innate, because what is truly innate to us is never absent from us.

Response

None of God's attributes can come from external objects as if they were a model or template, because there is nothing in God that resembles what we find in external, physical things. It is clear that whatever we think about God that differs from or is unlike what we observe in these external things does not originate from those things themselves, but rather from a cause that creates this very difference in our thinking.

And here I want to understand how this philosopher derives God's understanding from external things, yet I can easily explain what concept I have of it by saying that through the idea of God's understanding I conceive whatever constitutes the form of any perception. For who is there that does not perceive that he understands something or other, and consequently he must thereby have an idea of understanding, and by expanding it infinitely he forms the idea of God's understanding. And so it is with his other attributes.

Since we have used the idea of God that exists within us to prove his existence, and since this idea contains such immense power that we find it contradictory to think God could exist while anything else exists that he did not create, it clearly follows that in proving his existence we also prove that the entire world, or everything that is different from God, was created by God.

Finally, when we claim that certain ideas are innate or natural to us, we don't mean that they are constantly present in our minds (because if that were the case, no idea would truly be innate), but rather that we possess within ourselves the ability to generate them.

OBJECTION. XI.

The entire weight of this argument rests on the following point: I know it is impossible for me to possess the nature I have—namely, having the idea of God within me—unless God truly exists. I mean that very same God whose idea exists in my mind.

Since it has not been proven that we have an idea of God, and the Christian religion teaches us to believe that God is beyond human understanding—meaning, as I interpret it, that we cannot form an idea of Him—it follows that the existence of God has not been demonstrated, and even less so the Creation.

Response

When God is said to be inconceivable, this refers to having a complete and adequate understanding of Him. But I am growing weary of constantly repeating how we can still have an idea of God despite this. Therefore, nothing presented here contradicts my demonstration.

OBJECTION XII.

AGAINST THE FOURTH MEDITATION, OF TRUTH AND FALSEHOOD.

By this I mean that error (as error itself) is not a real entity that depends on God, but is simply a deficiency; and therefore for me to make mistakes, there is no need for God to have given me a special ability to err.

It's certain that ignorance is simply a lack of something, and that no positive ability is needed to make us ignorant. However, this idea isn't as clear when it comes to error, because stones and lifeless objects cannot make mistakes, and this is only because they don't possess the abilities to reason or imagine. From this, it's natural for us to conclude that making errors requires the ability to judge, or at least to imagine, and both of these abilities are positive qualities that are given to all creatures capable of error, and only to them.

Moreover, Descartes states that he finds his errors depend on two contributing causes: his faculty of knowing and his faculty of choosing, or the freedom of his will. This appears to contradict what he said earlier. We can also observe here that freedom of will is assumed without any proof, contrary to the opinion of the Calvinists.

Response

Although making us err requires a faculty of reasoning (or more precisely, of judging—that is, of affirming and denying) because error is a defect of this faculty, it doesn't follow that this defect is anything real, just as blindness isn't a real thing, even though stones cannot be called blind simply because they lack the capacity for sight. I'm quite surprised that in all these objections, I haven't found a single valid inference.

I haven't assumed anything here about the freedom of human will, except what everyone experiences within themselves and what is most clearly evident through natural understanding. I also don't see any reason why anyone would claim this contradicts any previous position.

Perhaps there are many people who, when considering God's predetermined arrangement of things, cannot understand how their freedom of will is compatible with it, but there is no person who, when considering only themselves, does not discover through experience that being willing and being free are one and the same thing. But this is not the place to investigate what others might think about this matter.

OBJECTION XIII.

For example, when I recently set myself to examine whether anything exists, and discovered that from my very act of examining such a question, it clearly follows that I myself exist, I could not help but judge what I so clearly understood to be true—not because I was compelled by any external force, but because a strong inclination in my will followed this great light in my understanding, so that I believed it all the more freely and willingly, the less indifferent I was to it.

This phrase, "Great Light in the Understanding," is metaphorical and therefore should not be used in logical arguments. Everyone who doesn't doubt their own opinion claims to have such enlightenment and feels just as compelled to assert what they believe as someone who actually and truly knows something. Therefore, this supposed light might cause someone to defend and stubbornly hold onto an opinion, but it can never be the source of truly knowing whether an opinion is correct.

Moreover, not only is the knowledge of truth independent of the will, but belief or giving assent are also not acts of the will; for whatever is proven by strong arguments, or credibly told, we believe whether we want to or not.

It's true that affirming or denying propositions, defending or opposing propositions, are acts of the will; but it doesn't follow from this that internal assent depends on the will. Therefore the following conclusion (that the misuse of our free will constitutes the deprivation that creates error) is not fully proven.

Response

It doesn't matter much whether this expression, "Great Light," is argumentative or not, as long as it serves to explain something, which it truly does. Everyone knows that when we speak of light in the understanding, we mean clarity of knowledge, which not everyone possesses who believes they do; and this doesn't prevent this light in the understanding from being very different from a stubborn opinion adopted without clear perception.

When it's stated here that we agree with things we clearly understand whether we want to or not, it's the same as saying that regardless of our wishes, we desire what we clearly recognize as good; however, the word "not wanting" has no place in such statements, because it suggests that we both want and don't want the same thing.

OBJECTION XIV.

AGAINST THE FIFTH MEDITATION. ON THE ESSENCE OF MATERIAL THINGS.

When I imagine a triangle, for instance, even though such a shape might not exist anywhere outside my thoughts and may never actually exist, its nature is still fixed, and its essence or form remains unchanging and eternal. This essence is not created by me and does not depend on my mind, as becomes clear from the fact that many propositions can be proven about this triangle.

If a triangle doesn't exist anywhere, I don't understand how it can have any nature, because something that exists nowhere simply isn't real, and therefore doesn't have being or any nature whatsoever.

The concept of a Triangle in our mind comes from seeing an actual triangle, or from combining elements we have previously observed, but once we assign the name "Triangle" to something (which we believe gives rise to our idea of a Triangle), even if that particular triangle is destroyed, the name itself remains. Similarly, once we understand that all the angles of a triangle equal two right angles, and we assign this additional description (namely, having three angles equal to two right angles) to a triangle, even if no such thing existed anywhere in the world, the name would still persist, and this statement, "A Triangle is a figure having three angles equal to two right angles," would remain eternally true. However, the essential nature of a triangle would not be eternal if every triangle were destroyed.

This statement, "A Man is an Animal," will remain true forever, because the word "Animal" will always mean what the word "Man" means; but certainly if humanity perishes, human nature will no longer exist.

From this it becomes clear that essence, when distinguished from existence, is nothing more than the joining of names through the word "is," and therefore essence without existence is merely a creation of our imagination. Just as the image of a person in the mind relates to an actual person, so essence relates to existence. Or to put it another way, just as the statement "Socrates is a man" relates to "Socrates is or exists," so the essence of Socrates relates to his existence. Now when we say "Socrates is a man" at a time when Socrates does not exist, this statement only signifies the connection between the names, and the word "is" carries with it the mental image of the unity of the thing that is called by these two names.

Response

The distinction between essence and existence is understood by everyone. What is discussed here regarding eternal names rather than eternal truth has already been thoroughly refuted long ago.

OBJECTION XV.

AGAINST THE SIXTH MEDITATION. OF THE EXISTENCE OF MATERIAL THINGS.

Since God has not given me the ability to determine whether these ideas come from physical bodies or not, but has instead given me a strong tendency to believe that these ideas are sent from physical bodies, I see no reason why God should not be considered a deceiver if these ideas came from anywhere other than corporeal beings, and therefore we must conclude that corporeal beings exist.

It's a commonly accepted belief that doctors who deceive their patients for the sake of their health, and fathers who deceive their children for their own good, are not guilty of any crimes by doing so, because the wrongness of deception doesn't lie in speaking false words, but rather in the harm caused to the person being deceived.

Let Descartes therefore consider whether this proposition, "God can under no circumstances deceive us," when taken universally, is true; for if it is not true when taken so universally, that conclusion, "Therefore corporeal beings exist," will not follow.

Response

It's not necessary for establishing my conclusion that we cannot be deceived under any circumstances (since I readily acknowledge that we may often be deceived), but rather that we cannot be deceived when our error would imply that God has a will to deceive us that would contradict his nature. And here again we find a faulty inference in this objection.

THE FINAL OBJECTION.

For now I clearly see a significant difference between them (that is sleep and waking) because my dreams are never connected by my memory with the other actions of my life.

I want to know whether it's certain that a person who is dreaming and questioning whether they are dreaming or not might also dream that they are connecting their dream to memories of things that happened long ago; if this is possible, then those actions from their past life could be considered just as real as if they were awake.

Moreover, because (as Descartes affirms) the certainty and truth of all knowledge depends only on the knowledge of the True God, either an atheist cannot conclude from the memory of his past life that he is awake, or else it is possible for a person to know that he is awake without the knowledge of the True God.

Response

A person who dreams cannot truly connect their dreams with memories of past events, though I admit they may dream that they are making such connections; after all, who has ever denied that someone can be deceived while asleep? But when they wake up, they can easily recognize their mistake.

An atheist might gather from memories of their past life that they are awake, but they cannot know that this indication is enough to make them certain they are not being deceived, unless they know they were created by a God who will not deceive them.

THE END

THANK YOU FOR READING

You've Just Read a Piece of the Greatest Library Ever Rebuilt

Thank you for reading.

This book is one of thousands we're restoring, reimagining, and translating as part of the **Modern Library of Alexandria** — a global movement to preserve and share humanity's most important ideas.

What was once lost to fire and time is now rising again — not just as memory, but as living, breathing knowledge, freely accessible to all.

What You Can Do Next:

- **Keep Reading.**

  Discover more legendary works — in beautiful print, audiobook, or digital form — at LibraryofAlexandria.com.

- **Build Your Own Library.**

  Every title is available as a paperback, hardcover, or collectible boxset — at true printing cost. Craft a personal library worthy of display.

- **Spread the Light.**

  Share this book. Tell others about the movement. Help us translate every timeless work into every language, so no reader is ever left behind.

By finishing this book, you've already taken part in something extraordinary.

Join us at LibraryofAlexandria.com

Together, we're rebuilding the greatest library the world has ever known.

With appreciation,

The Modern Library of Alexandria Team

Visit:
www.libraryofalexandria.com
Or scan the code below:

www.ingramcontent.com/pod-product-compliance
Lightning Source LLC
Chambersburg PA
CBHW011524240626
47154CB00009B/2965